F   MacDonald, George

Heather & Snow

4-1³

Victor Books by George MacDonald

A Quiet Neighborhood
The Seaboard Parish
The Vicar's Daughter
The Shopkeeper's Daughter
The Prodigal Apprentice
The Last Castle
On Tangled Paths
Heather and Snow

Winner Books by George MacDonald

The Boyhood of Ranald Bannerman
The Genius of Willie MacMichael
The Wanderings of Clare Skymer

HEATHER &SNOW

GEORGE MacDONALD

edited by
Elizabeth Guignard Hamilton

VICTOR BOOKS®

A DIVISION OF SCRIPTURE PRESS PUBLICATIONS INC.
USA CANADA ENGLAND

Heather and Snow was first published in England in 1893.

Library of Congress Catalog Card Number: 86-63158
ISBN: 0-89693-760-7

© 1987 by Elizabeth Guignard Hamilton
Printed in the United States of America

Cover illustration: Kenneth Call

VICTOR BOOKS
A division of Scripture Press Publications, Inc.
Wheaton, Illinois 60187

CONTENTS

EDITOR'S FOREWORD

George MacDonald was a forerunner of the Kaleyard School (cabbage patch school) of writing. This group of writers—including J.M. Barrie, Ian MacLaren, and S.R. Crockett—joined MacDonald in telling warmhearted tales about small villages and rural patches of Scotland. As in *Heather and Snow*, the action in the Kaleyard books often takes place almost entirely within a piece of Scotland only a few miles square.

Heather and Snow is the eighth George MacDonald novel from Victor Books. It originally appeared in 1893, and is one of his works that requires translation for the modern reader, as it was written in the broad Scots language. Much of the Scots has been translated or clarified; what remains gives the reader the flavor of the original. (Sometimes it helps to read the passages aloud.) Within *Heather and Snow*, the reader will encounter characters who express theological opinions that are not consonant with evangelical thought. This should not, however, deter the discriminating reader from appreciating the warm spiritual quality of the book.

George MacDonald's stories have continued to draw and teach me ever since I first began to read our battered copy of *Annals of a Quiet Neighborhood*. But some of MacDonald's heroes and heroines have seemed less than real to me, failing to enlist my sympathy with their problems. I simply could not identify with them: they were too perfect.

However, having edited two of his books and read many more, I have grown to be more sympathetic. In the world of heroes and heroines, we need to be able to look up to someone, to have an example to follow, to have a goal to strive for—and in today's world there are precious few examples of righteousness. When I learned that several of MacDonald's most admirable characters were based on real people that he knew and loved, I felt challenged. Why was I not like these people? Could I say that I would respond to similar situations with the same honesty and selflessness? Would I always seek another's welfare first? Could I be that sensitive to what Christ would have me do?

Almost one hundred years after they were written, MacDonald's words are still working, still challenging and sharpening. My wish for this edition of *Heather and Snow* is that its gentleness and simplicity will persuade each person who reads to listen with the heart to the age-old and ever-comforting message of our truest Hero, Jesus Christ.

Elizabeth Guignard Hamilton
Indianapolis, Indiana
December 1986

INTRODUCTION

George MacDonald (1824-1905), a Scottish preacher, poet, novelist, fantasist, expositor, and public figure, is most well known today for his children's books—*At the Back of the North Wind, The Princess and the Goblin, The Princess and Curdie,* and his fantasies *Lilith* and *Phantastes.*

But his fame is based on far more than his fantasies. His lifetime output of more than fifty popular books placed him in the same literary realm as Charles Dickens, Wilkie Collins, William Thackeray, and Thomas Carlyle. He numbered among his friends and acquaintances Lewis Carroll, Mark Twain, Lady Byron, and John Ruskin.

Among his later admirers were G.K. Chesterton, W.H. Auden, and C.S. Lewis. MacDonald's fantasy *Phantastes* was a turning point in Lewis' conversion; Lewis acknowledged MacDonald as his spiritual master, and declared that he had never written a book without quoting from MacDonald.

CHAPTER ONE

A Runaway Race

Upon two earthfast, neighboring stones, like islands in an ocean of heather, sat a boy and a girl. The girl was knitting or, as she would have called it, weaving a stocking; and the boy, his eyes fixed upon her face, was talking with an animation that amounted almost to excitement. He was very fluent, and could have talked just as fast in good English as in the dialect in which he was now pouring out his ambitions—the broad Saxon of Aberdeen.

He was telling the girl that he meant to be a soldier like his father, and quite as good a one as he. But he knew little of himself or the world, and with small genuine impulse to action, he was moved chiefly by the anticipated results of it. He saw success already his, and a grateful country at his feet.

"I'll not have the warld make lightly o' me!"

"Mebbe the warld willna tribble itself aboot ye as muckle as ye think!" returned his companion quietly.

"*Ye* do nothin ither!" retorted the boy, rising, and looking down on her in displeasure. "What for are ye aye teasin me? A body canna let his thoughts go, but ye're doon upo' them, like doves upo' corn!"

"I wouldna be teasin ye, Francie, but that I care over muckle aboot ye to let ye think I had the same opinion o' ye that ye have o' yerself," answered the girl, who went on with her knitting as she spoke.

"Ye'll never believe a body!" he rejoined, and turned half away. "I canna think what makes me keep comin to see ye! Ye havena a guid word to give a body!"

"It's none ye should get frae me, Francie! Ye think a heap over muckle o' yerself. What ye expect may some day come true, but ye have given nobody a right to expect it along wi' ye; I canna think if ye were fair to yerself, ye would count yerself one it was to be expected o'!"

"I told ye so, Kirsty! Ye never lay any weight upo' what a body says!"

"That depends upo' the body. Did ye never hear Maister Craig point oot the differ atween believin a body and believin *in* a body, Francie?"

"Na, and I dinna care."

"I wouldna like ye to go away thinkin I misdoobted yer word, Francie! I believe anythin ye tell me, as far as *I* think ye ken, but maybe no so far as *ye* think ye ken. I believe ye, but I confess I dinna believe *in* ye—yet. Ye're a guid rider and a guid shot for a laddie, and ye run middlin fast—I canna say like a deer, for I reckon I could lick ye myself at runnin! But, after and all—"

"Who's braggin noo, Kirsty?" cried the boy.

"Me," answered Kirsty, "and I'll do what I brag o'!" she added, throwing her stocking on the patch of green sward about the stone, and starting to her feet with a laugh. "Is 't to be uphill or along?"

They were near the foot of a hill to whose top went the heather, but along whose base, between the heather and the bogland below, lay an irregular belt of moss and grass, pretty clear of stones. The boy did not seem eager to accept the challenge.

"There's no guid in lickin a lassie!" he said with a shrug.

"There must be guid in tryin to do 't though, especially if ye were licked at 't!" returned the girl.

"What guid can there be in a body bein licked at anythin?"

"The guid o' havin a body's pride taken doon a wee."

"I'm no so sure o' the guid o' that! It would only keep ye from tryin again."

"Jist there's what yer pride is to ye, Francie! Ye must always be first, or ye'll no try! Ye'll never do nothin for fear o' no bein able to go on believin ye could do better nor any ither body! It's a sore pity ye willna have yer pride taken doon. Come, I'm ready for ye! Never mind that I'm a lassie—nobody'll ken!"

"Ye have no shoes!" objected the boy.

"Ye can put off yer own!"

"My feet's no so hard as yours!"

"Weel, I'll put on mine. They're here, such as they are. Ye see, I want them goin through the heather wi' Steenie. Straight up hill through the heather, and I'll put my shoes on!"

"I'm no so guid uphill."

"See there noo, Francie. Ye take yerself for verra courteous and honorable and generous, and all that. Oh, I ken all aboot it, and it's all verra weel so far as it goes, but what the better are ye for 't, when, all the time ye're despisin a body 'cause she's but a lassie, ye must have every advantage o' her, or ye willna give her a chance o' lickin ye! Here, I'll put on my shoes. They're twice the weight o' yours, and they dinna fit me!" And she reached to put them on.

The boy did not dare go on refusing. He feared what Kirsty would say next, but he relished nothing at all in the challenge. It was not fit for a man to run races with a girl; there were no laurels, nothing but laughter to be won by the victory over her, and in his heart he was not at all sure of beating Kirsty. She had always beaten him when they were children. Since then they had been at the parish school together, but there public opinion kept the boys and girls to their own special sports. Now they were both fifteen, and Kirsty had left school. Francis was going to grammar school at the country town. All the sense was on the side of the girl, and she had been doing her best to make the boy practical like herself—but without much success, although he was by no means a bad sort of fellow. He had not yet passed the stage in which an admirer feels himself in the same category with his hero. Many are content with themselves because they side with those whose ways they do not endeavor to follow. Such are most who call themselves Christians. If men admired themselves only for what they did, their conceit would be greatly moderated.

Kirsty put on her heavy hobnailed shoes which were much too large for her, having been made for her brother. She stood up tall, and putting her elbows back, said, "I'll give ye the start o' me up to yon stane wi' the heather growin' oot o' the top o' 't."

"Na, na. I'll have none o' that!" answered Francis. "Fair play to all!"

"Ye'd better take it!"

"Off wi' ye, or I willna run at all!" cried the boy, and away they went.

Kirsty contrived that he should have a little head start—how much from generosity, and how much from determination that there should be nothing doubtful in the result, cannot be said— and for a good many yards he kept it. But if Francis had looked back, he might have seen that Kirsty was not doing her best— that she was in fact restraining her speed. Presently she quickened her pace, and was rapidly lessening the distance between them when, becoming aware of her approach, Francis quickened his, and for a time there was no change in their relative positions. Then again she quickened her pace—with an ease which made her seem capable of accelerating indefinitely—and was rapidly overtaking him. But as she drew near, she saw he panted, and she assumed a greater speed still, and passing him swiftly, left him far behind, without once looking round or slackening her pace.

The moment she put a shoulder of the hill between them, Francis flung himself down on the ground. Kirsty had felt certain he would do so, and fancied she heard him flop among the heather. But she could not be sure, for her blood was making tunes in her head, and the wind was blowing in and out of her ears with a pleasant but deafening accompaniment. When she knew he could see her no longer, she stopped likewise and threw herself down, while she was determining whether she should leave him, or walk back at her leisure and let him see how little she felt the run. She came to the conclusion that it would be kinder to allow him to get over his discomfiture in private. So she rose, and went straight up the hill.

About halfway to the summit, she climbed a rock as if she were a goat, and looked all around her. Then she uttered a shrill, peculiar cry, and listened. No answer came. Getting down as easily as she had got up, she walked along the side of the hill, passing far above the spot where her defeated rival yet lay, and descended at length into a little hollow not far from where she and Francis had been sitting.

Standing in this hollow was a very small hut built of turf from the peat moss below, and rooted with sod on which the heather still stuck. It scarcely caught the eye because it was close to the color of the ground about it. Its walls and roof were so thick that, small as it looked, it was much smaller inside. Outside it could not have measured more than ten feet in length, eight in width, and seven in height. Kirsty and her brother, Steenie, with help from Francis Gordon, had built it for themselves two years before. Their father knew nothing of the scheme until one day, proud of their success, Steenie asked him to see their handiwork. He was so pleased with it that he made them a door, on which he put a lock.

"For though this be no the kind o' place to draw crook-fingered gentry," he said, "some gangrel body might creep in and make his bed i' 't, and that lock'll be enough to hold him oot, I'm thinkin."

He also cut a hole through the wall, and fitted it with a window that opened and shut, which was more than could be said of every window at the farmhouse.

Into this nest Kirsty went, and there remained until it began to grow dark. She had hoped to find her brother waiting for her; but although disappointed, she chose to wait until Francis Gordon should be well on his way to the castle. Then she crept out, and ran toward home.

When she got there, she found Steenie engrossed in a young horse their father had just bought. She would like to have mounted him at once, for she would ride any kind of animal able to carry her; but, as he had never yet been backed, her father would not permit her.

CHAPTER TWO

Mother and Son

Francis lay for some time thinking Kirsty was sure to come back to him, but half wishing she would not. He rose at length to see whether she was on the way, but no one was in sight. At once the place was aghast with loneliness, as it must indeed have looked to anyone not at peace with solitude. Having sent several ringing shouts vainly after Kirsty, he turned and, in the descending light of an autumn afternoon, set out on the rather weary long walk to his home.

After passing the farm where Kirsty lived, two miles brought him to an ancient turreted house on the top of a low hill. There his mother sat expecting him, ready to tyrannize over him as usual, even though he would be leaving her within a week.

"Where have you been all day, Frank?" she said.

"I've had a long walk," he answered.

"You've been to Corbyknowe!" she returned. "I know it by your eyes. I know it by their very color that you're going to deceive me. Now don't tell me you haven't been there. I shall not believe you."

"I haven't been near the place, mother," said Francis, but as he said it his face glowed with a heat that did not come from the fire. He was not naturally an untruthful boy, and what he said was correct, for he had passed the house half a mile away, but his words gave the impression that he had not been with any of the people of Corbyknowe. His mother objected to his visiting the farmer; but he knew instinctively she would have objected yet more to his spending half the day with Kirsty, whom she never mentioned, and whose existence she scarcely recognized. Little as she loved her son, Mrs. Gordon would have scorned to suspect him of preferring the society of such a girl to her own. In truth, however, there were very few of his acquaintance whose company Francis would not have chosen rather than his mother's—except when he was ill. She was generally good to him then.

"Well, this once I shall believe you," she answered, "and I am glad to be able. It is a painful thought to me, Frank, that my son should feel the smallest attraction to low company. I have told you twenty times that the man was nothing but a private in your father's regiment."

"He was my father's friend!" answered the boy.

"He tells you so, I do not doubt," returned his mother. "He was not likely to leave that mouldy old stone unturned."

The mother sat and the son stood before her, in a drawing room whose hundred-year-old furniture must once have looked very modern and newfangled under the high narrow windows, and within the thick walls. Without a fire it was always cold. The carpet was very dingy, and the mirrors were spotted. But the poverty of the room was the respectable poverty of age: old furniture had become fashionable just in time to save it from being replaced by its mistress by a show of costly ugliness. A good fire of mingled peat and coal burned bright in the barrel-fronted steel grate, and shone in the brass fender. The boy's face continued to look very red in the glow, but still its color came more from within than from without. He cherished the memory of his father, and loved his mother just a little.

"He has told me a great deal more about my father than you ever did, mother!" he answered.

"Well, he may have!" she returned. "Your father was not a young man when I married him, and they had been together through I don't know how many campaigns."

"And you say he was not my father's friend?"

"Not his *friend*, Frank; his servant—what do they call them—his orderly, I dare say, but certainly not his friend."

"Any man may be another's friend!"

"Not in the way you mean, not that his son should go and see him every other day! A dog may be a man's best friend, and so was Sergeant Barclay your father's—a very good friend that way, I don't doubt!"

"You said a moment ago he was but a private, and now you call him Sergeant Barclay!"

"Well, where's the difference?"

"To be made sergeant shows that he was not a common man. If he had been, he would not have been set over others!"

"Of course, he was then, and is now, a very respectable man. If he were not I should never have let you go and see him at all. But you must learn to behave like the gentleman you are, and that you never will, while you frequent the company of your inferiors. Your manners are already almost ruined, fit for no place but a farmhouse! There you are, standing on the side of your foot again! Old Barclay, I dare say, tells you no end of stories about your mother!"

"He always asks after you, mother, and then never mentions you."

She knew perfectly that the boy spoke the truth.

"Don't let me hear of your being there again before you go to school!" she said definitively. "By the time you come home next year, I trust your tastes will have improved. Go and make yourself tidy for dinner. A soldier's son must before everything attend to his dress."

Francis went to his room, feeling it absolutely impossible to have told his mother that he had been with Kirsty Barclay, that he had run a race with her, and that she had left him alone at the foot of the Horn. That he could not be open with his mother, no one who knew her unreasoning and stormy temper would have wondered at; but the pitiful boy, who did not like lying, actually congratulated himself that he had got through without telling a downright falsehood.

CHAPTER THREE

At the Foot of the Horn

The region was like a waste place in the troubled land of dreams. It has been likened to "the ill place, wi' the fire oot," but there was nothing to suggest the silence of once roaring flame, no half-molten rocks no huge, honeycombed scoriae, no depths within depths glooming mystery and ancient horror. All one could see was a wide stretch of damp-looking level, mostly of undetermined or low-toned color, with here and there a brighter green of a patch of some growing crop. Flat and wide, the eye found it difficult to rest upon it and not sweep hurriedly from border to border for lack of self-asserted object on which to alight. It looked low, but indeed lay high—the bases of the hills surrounding it were far above the sea. These hills, at this season a ring of dull brown high-heaved hummocks, appeared to make of it a huge circular basin, miles in diameter, over the rim of which peered the tops and peaks of mountains more distant. Up the side of the Horn, which was the loftiest in the ring, ran a drystane dyke, a stone wall of considerable size, climbing to the very top—an ugly thing which the eye could not avoid. Plentiful as were the stones ready for that poorest use of stones, division, there was nothing but the grouse to have rendered it worth the proprietor's while to erect such a boundary to his neighbor's property.

Some of the farms that bordered the hollow, each running a little way up the side of the basin, were as well cultivated as any in Scotland; but winter there claims the paramountcy, and yields to summer so few of his rights that the place looks forbidding, if not repulsive, to such as do not live in it. To love it, one must have been born there. In the summer it has the character of *bracing*, but can be such only to those who are pretty well braced already. It would soon brace the delicate of certain sorts with the bands of death.

The region is in constant danger of famine. If the snows come earlier than usual, the crops lie green under it, and no store of meal can be laid up in the cottages. And, if the snow lies deep there is the difficulty of conveying even the most basic of supplies. Of course, the cottages are but few, and may be seen here and there on the southerly slopes of the basin, but hardly one in its bottom.

It was now summer, and in a month or two the landscape would look more cheerful. The heather that covered the hills would no longer be dry and brown and in places black with fire, but a blaze of red purple, a rich mantle of bloom. Even now, early in July, the sun had little power. It would not have been warm had there been the least motion in the air, but on this morning there was absolute stillness; and although it was not easy for Kirsty to imagine any summer air other than warm, yet the wind's absence had not a little to do with the sense of luxurious life that now filled her heart. She sat on her favorite grassy slope near the foot of the cone-shaped Horn, looking over the level miles before her, and knitting away at a ribbed stocking of dark blue whose toe she had nearly finished, glad in the thought not of rest from her labor but of beginning the yet more important fellow-stocking. She had no need to watch her work to keep the loops right; but she was so careful that if she lived to be old and blind, she would knit better then than now. It was to her the perfect glory of a summer day, and her delight in the divine luxury was greater than that of many a poet dwelling in softer climes.

The spot where she sat was near the turf hut, and at every

shifting of a needle she would send a new glance over her world. She saw far more than a stranger would have seen. Intense spots of live white accentuated the view, opaque yet brilliant with the heads of cottongrass here and there in thin patches on the dark ground, for nearly the whole level was peat moss. Miles and miles of peat, differing in quality and varying in depth, lay between those hills—almost the only fuel of the region. In some spots it was very wet, water lying beneath and all through its substance. Other dark spots were the sides of holes where it had been dug, showing where it was drier. The black spaces on the hills, where the old heather had been burned so its roots might shoot afresh, fed the grouse with soft young sprouts. Now they looked like neglected spots where men cast stones and shards, but by and by would be covered with a tenderer green than the rest of the hillside. Kirsty could barely see the moorland birds whose cries were now and then punctuated with the distant bark of a sheepdog.

The prospect might have seemed altogether uninteresting, perhaps even ugly, but certainly Kirsty Barclay did not think it such. The girl was more than well satisfied with the world shell in which she found herself. At the moment she was basking bodily and spiritually in the sun, the air, the wide expanse—the hilltops' nearness to the heavens which yet they could not invade; the little breezes which every now and then awoke to assert their existence by immediately ceasing; and doubtless also, the knowledge that her stocking was nearly done, that her father and mother were but a mile or so away, that she knew where Steenie was, and that a cry would bring him to her feet. Each of these things bore a part in making Kirsty quiet with satisfaction. Kirsty knew well that there was a deeper cause of her peace, the same that is the root of life itself. Happiness always made her quiet; but had her bliss changed suddenly to sadness, Kirsty would have been quiet still. Whatever came to Kirsty seemed right, for there it was!

She was now sixteen. The only sign that she had any interest in her appearance showed in her blue silk neckerchief and her hair. Of a gentle medium brown, with a rippling tendency to curl, it was parted and drawn back from her face into a net of its own color. She wore a blue print wrapper, like that of a peasant woman, and a blue winsey petticoat, beyond which appeared her bare feet, lovely in shape, and brown in hue. The hem of the petticoat was a little torn, but not more than might seem admissable, considering the rough wear to which the garment was exposed. Kirsty grudged the time spent on her clothes. She made or mended them to wear them, not think about them.

Her forehead was wide and rather low, with straight eyebrows and gentle hazel eyes. Her nose was strong and a little irregular, but with sensitive nostrils. A decided and well-shaped chin dominated her bare brown neck and seemed to assert the superiority of the face over her whole body. Its chief expression was of strong repose, a sweet, powerful peace, requiring but occasion to pass into determination.

If one could see the mind of a woman as she sits spinning or weaving, it would reveal the process next highest to creation. But the only hope of ever understanding such things lies in growing oneself. Be it soft as a moonlit night of reverie, or in a storm with tempest and lightning abroad, the enlarging by great bursts of vision and leaps of understanding and resolve, the story of God's universe lies in the growth of the individual soul. Kirsty's growth had been as yet quiet and steady.

Once more as she shifted her needle, her glance went flitting over the waste before her. This time there was more life in sight. Far away Kirsty saw a man upon a horse; to say how far would have been as difficult for one unused to the flat moor as for a landsman to reckon distances at sea. At length, after she had looked many times, she could clearly distinguish a youth on a strong handsome pony, and remained no longer in the slightest doubt as to who he might be.

They came steadily over the dark surface of the moor, and it was clear that the pony must know the nature of the ground well. He glided as fast as he could gallop, now made a succession of short jumps, now halted, examined the ground, and began slowly picking his way.

Kirsty watched his approach with gentle interest, while every movement of the youth indicated eagerness. Francis Gordon had seen her on the hillside, probably long before she saw him, had been coming to her in as straight a line as the ground would permit, and at length was out of the boggy level and ascending the slope of the hill to where she sat. When he was within twenty yards of her, she gave him a little nod and then fixed her eyes on her knitting. He held on till within a few feet of her, then pulled up and threw himself from his pony's back. The creature, covered with foam, stood a minute panting, then fell to work on the stout grass.

Francis had grown considerably, and looked almost a young man. Although he was a little older than Kirsty, he did not appear so, his expression being considerably younger than hers. Whether self-indugence or aspiration was to come out of his evident joy in life seemed yet undetermined. His countenance indicated nothing bad. He might well have represented one at the point before having to choose whether to go up hill or down. He was dressed a little showily in a short coat of dark tartan, and a highland bonnet with a brooch and feather, and carried a lady's riding whip—his mother's, no doubt—its top set with stones—so that his appearance was altogether a contrast to that of the girl. She was a peasant, he a gentleman! Her bare head and yet more bare feet emphasized the contrast. But which was by nature the superior, no one with the least insight could have doubted.

He stood and looked at her, but neither spoke. She cast at length a glance upward, and said, "Weel?"

Francis did not open his mouth. He seemed irresolute. Nothing in Kirsty's look or carriage or in the tone of her one word gave sign of consciousness that she was treating him strangely. With complete self-possession, she left the initiative to the one who had sought the interview; let him say why he had come!

Displeasure grew in his face. Two or three times he turned half away with the movement instantly checked which seemed to say that in a moment more, if there came no change, he would mount and ride. Was this all his welcome?

At last she appeared to think she must take mercy on him. He used to say thirty words to her one!

"That's a bonny powny ye have," she remarked, with a look at the creature as he fed.

"He's that," he answered dryly.

"Where did ye get him?" she asked.

"My mither bought him for my hamecomin," he replied. He paused. "He's a bonny creature and willin. He'll go through anythin—water anyway—I'm no so sure aboot fire. His name's Don."

A long silence followed, broken this time by the youth.

"Won't ye give me luik nor word, and me ridin' like mad to have a sight o' ye?" he said.

She glanced up at him.

"Weel, ye have that!" she answered, with a smile that showed her lovely white teeth. "Ye're all bemired! What for should ye be in sic a hurry? Ye saw me no three days ago!"

"Ay, I saw ye. But I dinna get a word o' ye!"

"Ye was free to say what ye liked. There was none but my mither!"

"Would ye have me say anythin afore yer mither jist as I would if ye were alone?" he asked.

"Ay would I," she returned. "Since she would ken, withoot my havin to tell her, what a goose as ye was!"

Had he not seen the sunny smile that accompanied her words, he might well have taken offense.

"I wish ye were anither sic like!" he answered simply.

"Then there would be two o' us!" she returned, leaving him to interpret.

Silence again fell.

"Weel, what would ye have, Francie?" said Kirsty at length.

"I would have ye promise to marry me, Kirsty, come the time," he answered. "And ye ken as well as I when that would be."

"That's straight oot!" retorted Kirsty. "But ye see, Francie," she went on, "yer father, when he left ye as a kind o' legacy to my father, had no intention that *I* was to be left oot. Neither had *my* father when he accepted it!"

"I dinna understand ye one atom!" interrupted Francie.

"Hold yer tongue and hearken," returned Kirsty. "What I'm meanin's this: what lies to my father's hand lies to mine as weel, and I'll never have it said that when my father pulled one way, I pulled anither!"

"Sakes, lassie! What *are* ye gettin at? Would it be pullin against yer father to marry me?"

"It would be that."

"I dinna see how ye can make it oot! I dinna see how, bein sic a friend o' my father's, he should object to my father's son!"

"Eh, but laddies *are* gowks!" cried Kirsty. "My father was your father's friend for *his* sake, no for his own! He thinks o' what would be guid for you, no for himself!"

"Weel, but," persisted Gordon, "it would be more for my guid nor anything he could wish for, to have you for my wife!"

Kirsty's nostrils began to quiver, and her lips rose in a curve of scorn.

"A bonny wife ye would have, Francie Gordon," she replied, "who kennin her father doin each mortal thing for the love o' his old maister and comrade, took the fine chance to make her own o' 't! That my father had a lass-bairn o' his ain showed more nor anythin the trust your father put in 'im! Francie, the verra grave would cast me oot for shame that I should once have thought o' sic a thing! Man, it would almost drive yer lady-mither demented!"

"It's my business, Kirsty, who I marry!"

"And I hope ye'll allow it's part *my* business who ye shall *not* marry—and that's me, Francie!"

He sprang to his feet with a look of wrath and despair that for a moment frightened Kirsty. She thought of the terrible bog holes on the way Francis had come. She sprang also to her feet and caught him by the arm where, his foot already in the stirrup, he stood in the act of mounting.

"Francie! Francie!" she cried. "Hearken to reason! There's no a body, man or woman, I like better nor yerself to do ye any turn o' guid—'cept my father, of course, and my mither, and my ain Steenie!"

"And how many more, if I had the will to hear the long Bible chapter o' them, and see myself comin in at the tail o' them all? Na, na! It's time I was home. If ye had a score o' idiot brithers, ye would care more for each one o' them nor for me! I canna bide to think o' 't."

"It's true all the same, whether ye can bide to think o' 't or no, Francie!" returned the girl, her face, which had been very pale, now rosy with indignation. "My Steenie's more to me nor all the Gordons thegither!"

She drew back, sat down again to the stocking she was knitting for Steenie, and left him to mount and ride, which he did without another word.

"There's more nor one kind o' idiot," she said to herself, "and Steenie's no the kind that ought to be called one. There's more in Steenie than in six Francie Gordons!"

If ever Kirsty came to love a man, it would be nothing to her to die for him, but then it never would have been anything to her to die for her father or her mother or Steenie!

Gordon galloped off at a wild pace, as if he would drive his pony straight athwart the terrible moss. But glancing behind and seeing that Kirsty was not looking after him, he turned the creature's head in a safer direction, and left the moss at his back.

CHAPTER FOUR

Dog Steenie

Kirsty sat for some time at the foot of the hill, motionless as itself save for her hands. The sun shone on in silence, and the blue butterflies which haunted the little bush of bluebells beside her made no noise. Only a stray bee, happy in the pale heat, made a little music to please itself. Kirsty had an unusual power of sitting still, even with nothing for her hands to do. On the present occasion, however, her hands and fingers went faster than usual, not entirely from eagerness to finish her stocking, but partly from her displeasure with Francis. At last she broke her worset, drew the end of it through the final loop, and, drawing it, rose and scanned the side of the hill. Not far off she spied the fleecy backs of a few feeding sheep, and straightway sent out on the still air a sweet, strong, musical cry. It was instantly responded to by a bark from somewhere up the hill. She sat down, clasped her hands over her knees, and waited.

She had not long to wait. A sound of rushing came through the heather, and in a moment or two, a fine collie, with a long, silky, wavy coat of black and brown, and one white spot on his face, shot out of the heather, sprang upon her, and, setting his paws on her shoulders, began licking her face. She threw her arms around him, and addressed him in words of fondling rebuke.

"Ye ill-mannered tyke!" she said. "What right have ye to take the place o' yer betters? Get doon wi' ye, and wait. What for should ye take advantage o' your four legs to his twa, and him the maister o' ye! But, eh Snootie, ye're a fine doggie, and I canna bide the thought that yer longest day must be so short, and take ye away home so long afore the rest o' us!"

While she scolded, she let him caress her as he pleased. Presently he left her, and going a yard or two away, threw himself on the grass with such abandon as no animal but a weary dog seems capable of reaching. He had made haste to be first that he might caress her before his master came; now he heard him close behind and knew his opportunity over.

Stephen came next out of the heather, creeping to Kirsty's feet on all fours. He was a gaunt, long-backed lad who at undetermined times either imagined himself the animal he imitated, or had some notion of being compelled to behave like a dog. When the fit was upon him, all day long he would speak no word even to his sister, and would only bark or give a low growl like the collie. In this last, he succeeded much better than in running like Snootie. He let his head hang low as he went, throwing it up to bark, and sinking it yet lower when he growled, which was seldom, and to those that loved him indicated great trouble. Unlike Snootie, he did not raise himself on his hind legs to caress his sister, but gently subsided upon her feet, and there lay panting, his face to the earth and his forearms crossed beneath his nose.

Kirsty stooped, and stroked and patted him as if he were the dog he seemed. Then drawing her feet from under him, she rose, and going a little way up the hill to the hut, returned presently with a basin full of rich milk, and a piece of thick oatcake which she had brought from home in the morning. She set the milk beside her as she resumed her seat; then she put her feet under the would-be dog, and proceeded to break small pieces from the oatcake and throw them to him. He sought every piece eagerly as it fell, but with his mouth only, never moving either hand, and seemed to eat with a satisfaction worthy of his simulated nature. When the oatcake was gone, she set the bowl before him, and he drank the milk with care and neatness, never putting a hand to steady it.

"Now you must have a sleep, Steenie!" said his sister.

She rose, and he crawled slowly after her up the hill on his hands and knees. All the time he kept his face down, and, his head hanging toward the earth, his long hair hid it quite. He strongly suggested a great Skye terrier.

When they reached the hut, Kirsty went in and Steenie crept after her. They had covered the floor with heather, the stalks upright and close packed, so that even where the bells were worn off, it still made a thick, long-piled carpet, elastic and warm. When the door was shut, they were snug there even in winter.

Inside, the hut was about six feet long, and four wide. Its furniture was a little deal table and one low chair. In the turf wall, at the opposite end from the door, Kirsty had cut out a small oblong recess to serve as a shelf for her books. The hut was indeed her library, for in that bole, in proper and tidy fashion, was almost every book she could call her own. There were about a dozen, several with but one board and some with no title, one or two very old, and all well used. When she was not knitting, Kirsty spent most of her time reading and thinking about what she read. Among her treasures was a curious old book of ghost stories, concerning which the sole remark she was ever heard to make was that she would like to know whether they were true; she thought Steenie could tell, but she would not question him about them. Ramsay's *Gentle Shepherd* was there, which she liked for the good sense in it. There was a thumbed edition of Burns also, but much of the thumbing was not Kirsty's, though she knew several of his best poems by heart.

Between the ages of ten and fifteen, Kirsty had gone to the parish school of the nearest town, Tiltowie. It looked like a village, but they always called it *the town*. There an aunt lived, and with her Kirsty was welcome to spend the night, so that she was able to go in most weather. But when she stayed there, her evening was mostly spent at the schoolmaster's.

Mr. Colin Craig was an elderly man who had married late and

lost his wife early. She had left him one child, a delicate, dainty, golden-haired thing, considerably younger than Kirsty, who cherished a maternal love and protection for her. Little Phemy would not have learned a thing but for Kirsty. Her father was never able to see in her anything but the little girl his wife had left him. He spoiled her a good deal, and never set himself to instruct her, leaving it apparently to the tendency of things to make of her a woman like her mother.

He was a real student and excellent teacher. When he first came as schoolmaster to Tiltowie, he was a divinity student, but a man so far of original thought that he saw lions in the way of becoming a minister. Such men as would be servants of the church before they are servants of the church's Master will never be troubled with Mr. Craig's difficulties. For one thing, his strong poetic nature made it impossible for him to believe in a dull, prosaic God; when told that God's thoughts are not as our thoughts, he found himself unable to imagine them inferior to ours. The natural result was that he remained a schoolmaster, to the advantage of many a pupil, and very greatly to the advantage of Kirsty, whose nature was peculiarly open to his influences. The schoolmaster said he had never had a pupil that gave him such satisfaction as Kirsty. She seemed to anticipate and catch at everything he wanted to make hers, and he declared that there was no knowledge he could offer which the lassie from Corbyknowe would not take in like her porridge. Best thing of all for her was that in his English class he paid far more attention to poetry than prose. Colin Craig was himself a master of the more recondite forms of verse. If, in some measure led astray by the merit of the form, he was capable of admiring inferior verses, yet he certainly admired the better poetry more.

In a word, Kirsty learned everything Mr. Craig brought within her reach; and long after she left school, the Saturday on which she did not go to see him was a day of disappointment both to the teacher and his little Phemy.

When she had once begun to follow a thing, Kirsty would never leave its trail. Her chief business as well as delight was to look after Steenie; but perfect attention to him left her large opportunity of pursuing her studies, especially at such seasons in which his peculiar affliction, whatever it really was, required hours of untimely sleep. Although at all times he wandered at his will without her, he invariably wanted to be near her when he slept. Satisfied that he slept better near her, she had not once at such a time left him. During summer, and as long before and after as the temperature permitted, the hut was the place he preferred for sleep; and it was Kirsty's special delight to sit in it on a warm day, the door open and her brother asleep on her feet, reading and reading while the sun went down the sky, to fill the hut as he set with a glory of promise. During the long gloaming, like a life out of which the light but not the love has vanished, she neither worked nor read, but brooded over many things.

Now, leaving the door open behind them, Kirsty took a book from the bole, and seated herself on a low chair. Steenie, who had waited motionless until she was settled, threw himself across her feet on the carpet of heather, and in a moment was fast asleep.

There they remained, the one reading, the other sleeping, while the hours of the warm summer afternoon slipped away, ripples on the ocean of the lovely, changeless eternity, the consciousness of God. For a time the watching sister was absorbed in *King Lear*. At last she drew her bare feet from under Steenie and put them on his back, where the coolness was delightful. Then first she became aware that the sun was almost down and the gloaming come, and that the whole world must be feeling just like her feet. The afternoon shadows had lengthened, and the eerie sleeping day, when the lovely ghosts come out of their graves in the long grass and walk about in the cool world, was slipping away. Kirsty was always willing to believe in ghosts. In her twilight reveries, she grew very nearly a ghost herself.

It was a wonder she could sit so long and not feel worn out, but Kirsty was exceptionally strong, in absolute health, and specially gifted with patience. Early in life she had so firmly grasped the idea that she was sent into the world expressly to take care of Steenie, that devotion to him had grown into a happy habit with her. The waking mind gave itself up to the sleeping, the orderly brain to the troubled, the true heart to the one as true.

CHAPTER FIVE

Colonel and Sergeant

There was no difference of feeling between David and Marion Barclay in regard to Kirsty's devotion to her Steenie, but the mother especially was content with it. While Kirsty was the apple of her eye, Steenie was her one loved anxiety.

David, like his father and grandfather and many more of the ancestors, was born on the same farm he now occupied. While his father was still alive, and with an elder son to succeed him, David enlisted—mainly from a strong desire to be near a school friend, then an ensign in the service of the East India Company. Throughout their following military career they were in the same regiment, the one rising to be colonel, the other sergeant major. All the time, the schoolboy attachment went on deepening in the men; and, all the time, was never man more respectfully obedient to orders than David Barclay to those of the superior officer with whom, in private, he was on terms of intimacy. As often as they could without attracting notice, the comrades threw aside all distinction of rank, and were again the Archie Gordon and Davie Barclay of old schooldays—as real to them still as those of the hardest battles they had fought together. In more primitive Scotland, such relations were more possible than in countries where more divergent habits of life occasion wider social separations; and then too, these were sober-minded men, who neither made much of the shows of the world, nor were greedy after distinction, which is the mere coffin wherein duty-done lies buried.

When they returned to their country, both somewhat disabled, the one retired to his inherited estate, the other to the family farm upon that estate, where his brother had died shortly before; so that Archie was now Davie's landlord. But no new relation would ever destroy the friendship which school had made close and war had welded. Almost every week the friends met and spent an evening together—much oftener at Corbyknowe than at Castle Weelset. For both married soon after their return, and their wives were of different natures.

"My colonel has the glory," Barclay said once to his sister, "but, poor fellow, I have the wife!" And truly the wife at the farm had in her material enough, both moral and intellectual, for ten ladies better than the wife at the castle.

David's wife brought him a son, Steenie, the first year of their marriage, and the next year came a son to the colonel and a daughter to the sergeant. One night, as the two fathers sat together at the farm, some twelve hours after the birth of David's girl, they mutually promised that the survivor would do his best for the child of the other. Before he died the colonel would gladly have taken his boy from his wife and given him to his old comrade.

While his wife was awaiting Steenie, David met with a rather serious accident with a young horse in the harvest field, and a report reached his young wife that he had been killed. To the shock she thus received, before she learned the truth, was generally attributed the peculiarity of the child, prematurely born within a month after. He had long passed the age at which children usually begin to walk, before he would even attempt to stand, but he had grown capable of a speed on all fours that was astonishing. When at last he did walk, it was for more than two years with the air of one who had learned a trick; and throughout a great part of his boyhood, he continued to go on all fours rather than on his feet.

CHAPTER SIX

Man Steenie

The afternoon shadows lengthened outside the hut, and Kirsty had put her book down long before the sleeping youth began at length to stir, but it was more than an hour before he quite woke up. Then all at once he started to his feet with his eyes wide open, putting back from his forehead the long hair which fell over them, and revealing a face not actually looking old but strongly suggesting age. His eyes were of a pale blue, with a hazy, uncertain gleam in them, reminding one of the shifty shudder and shake and start of the northern lights at some heavenly version of the game of Puss in the Corner. His features were more than good; they would have been grand had they been large, but they were peculiarly small. His head itself was very small in proportion to his height, but his forehead was large and his chin was strong. Although he had been all day acting a dog in charge of sheep, and treating the collie as his natural companion, there was in his countenance a remarkable absence of the animal. He had a kind of exaltation in his look; he seemed to expect something, not at hand but sure to come. With a look of absolute devotion, his eyes rested for a moment on the face of his sister; then he knelt at her feet, as if to receive her blessing, and bowed his head before her. She laid her hand upon it, and in a tone of unutterable tenderness said, "Man Steenie!" Instantly he rose to his feet. Kirsty rose also, and they went out of the hut.

The sunlight had not left the west, but had crept round some distance toward the north. Stars were shining faintly through the thin shadow of the world. Steenie stretched himself up, threw his arms aloft and held them raised, as if he would reach toward the infinite. Then he looked down on Kirsty, for he was taller than she, and pointed straight up, with the long forefinger of one of the long lean arms that had all day been legs to the would-be dog, and smiled. Kirsty looked up, nodded her head, and smiled in return. Then they started in the direction of home, and for some time walked in silence. At length Steenie spoke. His voice was rather feeble, but clear, articulate, and musical.

"My feet's terrible heavy the night, Kirsty!" he said. "If it wasna for them, the rest o' me would be up and away. It's terrible to be holden doon by the feet this way!"

"We're all holden doon the same way, Steenie. Maybe it's some worse for you that you would so fain go up, than for the rest o' us that's more willin to bide a wee. But it'll be the same at last when we're all up there thegither."

"I wouldna care so muckle if He didna grip me by the ankles, like! I dinna like to be gripped by the ankles! He willna let me in wi' the thongs!"

"When the right time comes," returned Kirsty solemnly, "the Bonny Man'll loose the thongs Himself."

"Ay, ay! I ken that weel. I'm thinkin I'll see Him the night, for I'm sore holden doon, sore needin a sight o' Him!"

"I dinna wonder that ye're so fain to see Him, Steenie!"

"I *am* that—fain, fain!"

"Ye'll see Him afore long. It's a fine thing to have patience."

"Ye come every day, Kirsty. What for shouldna He come every night?"

"He has reasons, Steenie. He kens best."

"Ay, He kens best. I ken nothin but Him—and you, Kirsty!"

Kirsty said no more. Her heart was too full.

Steenie stood still, and throwing back his head, stared for

some moments up into the great heavens over him. Then he spoke. "It's a bonny day, the day the Bonny Man bides in! The ither day—the day the rest o' ye bides in—the day when I'm no myself but a sore uncomfortable collie—that day's over hot and sometimes over cold; but the day He bides in is aye jist what a day should be! Ay, it's that! It's that!"

He threw himself down, and lay for a minute looking up into the sky. Kirsty stood and regarded him with loving eyes.

"I have all the bonny day afore me!" he murmured to himself. "Eh, but it's better to be a man nor a beast. Snootie's a fine beast and a grand collie, but I would raither be myself—a heap raither—always at hand to catch a sight o' the Bonny Man! Ye must go hame til yer bed, Kirsty! Is 't the Bonny Man comes til ye in yer dreams and says, 'Go til him, Kirsty, and be mortal guid til him?' It must be surely that!"

"Willna ye go wi' me, Steenie, as far as the door?" rejoined Kirsty, almost beseechingly, and attempting no answer to what he had last said.

It was at times such as this that Kirsty knew sadness. When she had to leave her brother on the hillside all the long night, to look on no human face, hear no human word, but wander in strangest worlds of his own throughout the slow dark hours, the sense of a separation worse than death would wrap her as in a shroud. When he was near, however far away in thought or sleep or dreams his soul might be, she could yet tend him with her love; but when he was out of her sight, and she had to sleep and forget him, where was Steenie, and how was he faring? Then he seemed to her as one forsaken, left alone with his sorrows to an existence companionless and dreary.

But, in truth, Steenie was by no means to be pitied. However much his life was apart from the lives of other men, he did not therefore live alone. Was he not still of more value than many sparrows? And Kirsty's love for him had in it no shadow of despair. Her pain at such times was but the indescribable love-lack of mothers when their sons are far away and they do not know what they are doing, what they are thinking; or when their daughters seem to have departed from them forever. And yet how few, when the air of this world is clearest, ever come into essential contact with those they love best. But the triumph of Love, while most it seems to delay, is yet ceaselessly rushing hitherward on the wings of the morning.

"Willna ye go as far as the door wi' me, Steenie?" she said again.

"I will do that, Kirsty. But ye're no feared, are ye?"

"Na, no a grain! What would I be feared for?"

"Ow, nothin! There's nothin oot and aboot to be feared at. In what ye call the daytime, I'm kind o' in danger o' knockin myself again' things. I never do that at night."

As he spoke he sprang to his feet, and they walked on. Kirsty's heart seemed to swell with pain, for Steenie was at once more rational and more strange than usual, and she felt the further away from him. His words were very quiet, but his eyes looked full of stars.

"I canna tell what it is aboot the sun that makes a dog o' me!" he said. "He holds me oot and makes me hang my head and feel as if I were kind o' ashamed, though I ken o' nothin. But the bonny night comes straight up til me, and intil me, and goes all through me, and bides i' me, and since I look for the Bonny Man!"

"I wish ye would let me bide oot the night wi' ye, Steenie!"

"What for that, Kirsty! Ye must sleep, and I'm better alone."

"That's jist it!" returned Kirsty, with a deep-drawn sigh. "I canna bide yer bein alone, and yet, do what I like, I canna, even i' the daytime, be a bit nearer til ye! If only ye was as little as ye used to be, when I could carry ye aboot all day, and take ye intil my own bed at night! But noo we're jist like the sun and the moon! When ye're oot, I'm in, and when ye're in—well, I'm no oot, but my soul's jist as blear-faced as the moon i' the daylight to think ye'll be away again so soon! But it *canna* go on like this til all eternity, and that's a comfort!"

"I ken nothin aboot eternity. I'm thinkin it'll all turn intil a long starry night, wi' the Bonny Man in 't. I'm sure o' one thing, and that only—that somethin'll be put right that's far from right the noo, and since, Kirsty, ye'll have yer own way wi' me, and I'll be so far like ither fowk. Idiot that I am, I would be sorry to be turned althegither the same as some! Ye see I ken so muckle they ken nothin aboot, or they wouldna be as they are! It maybe doesna become *me* to say 't, any more nor Gowk Murnock that sits on the pulpit stair, but the nonsense our minister dings oot o' his own head, as if it were the story oot o' the Bible! It's no possible he's ever seen the Bonny Man as I have seen Him!"

"We'll all have to come over til you, Steenie, and learn from what ye ken. We'll have to make *you* the minister, Steenie!"

"Na, na. I ken nothin for ither fowk—only for myself!"

"Some night ye'll let me bide oot wi' ye all night? I would so like it, Steenie!"

"Ye shall, Kirsty, but it must be some night ye have sleeped all day."

"Eh, but I couldna do that, tried I ever so hard!"

"Ye could lie i' yer bed anyway, and make the best o' it!"

They went all the rest of the way talking like this, and Kirsty's heart grew light, for she seemed to get a little nearer to her brother. He had been her live doll ever since his mother had laid him in her arms when she was little more than three years old. For though Steenie was nearly a year older than Kirsty, she was at that time so much bigger that she was able not, indeed, to carry him but to nurse him on her knees. She thought herself the elder of the two until she was about ten, by which time she could not remember any beginning to her carrying of him. About the same time, however, he began to grow much faster, and she found before long that she could only carry him upon her back for any distance.

The discovery that he was the elder somehow gave a fresh impulse to her love and devotion, and intensified her pitiful tenderness. Kirsty's was indeed a heart in which the whole unhappy world might have sought and found shelter. She had the notion, notwithstanding, that she was harder-hearted than most, and therefore better able to do the things that were right but not pleasant.

CHAPTER SEVEN

Corbyknowe

"Ye'll come in and say a word to mither, Steenie?" said Kirsty, as they came near the door of the house.

It was a long, low building, with a narrow path of paving stones in front from end to end. Its walls, rough cast and white washed, shone dim in the twilight. Under a thick projecting thatch the door stood wide open; and from the kitchen, whose door was also open, came the light of a peat fire and a fish oil lamp. Throughout the summer Steenie was seldom in the house an hour of the twenty-four, and now he hesitated to enter. In the winter he would stay about it a good part of the day, and was generally indoors the greater part of the night, but by no means always.

While he hesitated, his mother appeared in the doorway of the kitchen. She was a tall fine-looking woman, with soft gray eyes, and an expression of form and features which left Kirsty accounted for.

"Come in, Steenie, my man!" she said, in a tone that seemed to wrap its object in fold upon fold of tenderness, enough to make the peat smoke that pervaded the kitchen seem the very atmosphere of the heavenly countries. "Come and have a drappy o' new milk, and a piece o' bread."

Steenie stood smiling and undecided on the slab in front of

the doorstep.

"Dread nothin, Steenie," his mother went on. "There's no one to interfere wi' yer will, whatever it be. The hoose is yer own to come and go as ye see fit. But ye ken that, and Kirsty kens that, as weel's yer father and myself."

"Mither, I ken what ye say to be the truth. A body believes their own mither—that's in the order o' things as they were first started! Still I would raither no come in the night. I would raither hold away and no tribble ye wi' more o' the sight o' me nor I can help. I dinna ken what I'm aboot, but I ken that I'm a kind o' disgrace to ye, though I canna tell hoo I'm to blame for 't. So I'll jist bide theroot wi' the bonny stars that's aye theroot, and kens all aboot it, and doesna think none the worse o' me."

"Laddie! Laddie! Who on the face o' God's earth thinks the worse o' ye for a wrong done ye? Though who had the blame o' that I darena think, weel kennin that a thing's aither ordeened or allowed, makin' muckle the same. Come winter, come summer, come right, come wrong, come life, come death, what are ye, what can ye be, but my ain, ain, laddie!"

Steenie stepped across the threshold and followed his mother into the kitchen, where the pot was already on the fire for the evening's porridge. To hide her emotion she went straight to it, and lifted the lid to look whether it was boiling. Just then the stalwart form of her husband appeared in the doorway, and there stood for a single moment arrested.

He was a good deal older than his wife, as his long gray hair testified. He was six feet in height, with a rather stiff, military carriage. His face wore an expression of stern goodwill, as if he had been sent to do his best for everybody, and knew it.

Steenie caught sight of him ere he had taken a step into the kitchen. He rushed to him, threw his arms round him, and hid his face on his bosom. "Bonny, bonny man!" he murmured, then turned away and went back to the fire.

His mother was casting the first handful of meal into the pot. Steenie fetched a three-legged stool and sat down by her, looking as if he had sat there every night since he was first able to sit.

The farmer came forward, and drew a chair to the fire beside his son. Steenie laid his head on his father's knee, and the father laid his big hand on Steenie's head. Not a word was uttered. The mother might have found them in the way had she been so inclined, but the thought did not come to her, and she went on making the porridge in great contentment, while Kirsty laid the cloth. The night was as still in the house as in the world, save for the bursting of the big blobs of the porridge. The peat fire made no noise.

The mother at length took the heavy pot from the fire, and with what seemed wonderful skill, poured the porridge into a huge wooden bowl on the table. Having then scraped the pot carefully that nothing shoud be lost, she put some water in it, and setting it on the fire again, placed two eggs gently in the water.

She went to the dairy and, returning with a jug of the richest milk, set it beside the porridge, whereupon they drew their seats to the table—all but Steenie.

"Come, Steenie," said his mother, "here's yer supper."

"I dinna care aboot any supper the night, mither," answered Steenie.

"Guidsake, laddie, I kenna hoo ye live!" she returned in an accent almost of despair.

"I'm thinkin I dinna need so muckle as ither fowk," rejoined Steenie, whose white face bore testimony that he took far from enough nourishment. "Ye see I'm no all there," he added with a smile. "So I canna need so muckle!"

"There's enough o' ye there to fill my heart verra full," answered his mother with a deep sigh. "Come on, Steenie, my bairn!" she went on coaxingly. "Yer father willna eat a mouthful if ye dinna—ye'll see that! Eh, Steenie," she broke out, "if ye would but take yer supper and go to yer bed like the rest o' us! It makes my heart swell as if 't would burst like a blob to think o' ye oot i' the mirk night! Who's to tell what mightna be happenin to ye!"

"I'll bide in, if that be yer will," replied Steenie. "But eh, if ye kenned the differ til me, ye wouldna wish 't. I seldom sleep at night as ye ken, and i' the hoose it's jist as if the darkness went inside o' me and was chokin me."

"But it's as dark theroot as i' the house!"

"Na, mither. It's never so dark theroot but there's light enough to ken *I'm* theroot and no i' the hoose. I can always draw a guid full breath oot i' the open."

"Let the laddie go his own way," interposed David. "The thing born in 'im 's better for him nor the thing born in anither. A man must go as God made 'im."

"Ay, whether he be man or dog!" assented Steenie solemnly.

He drew his stool close to his father where he sat at the table, and again laid his head on his knee. The mother sighed but said nothing. She looked nowise hurt, only very sad. In a minute, Steenie spoke again.

"I'm thinkin none o' ye kens," he said, "what it's like when all the hillside's given up to the ither ones!"

"What ither ones?" asked his mother. "There can be none there but yer ain lone self!"

"Ay, there's all the rest o' us," he rejoined, with a wan smile.

The mother looked at him with something almost of fear in her eyes of love.

"Steenie has company we ken little aboot," said Kirsty. "I think I would give him my wits for his company."

"Ay, the Bonny Man!" murmured Steenie. "I must be goin!"

But he did not rise, did not even lift his head from his father's knee. It would be rude to go before the supper was over—the ruder that he was not partaking of it!

David had eaten his porridge, and now came the almost nightly difference about the eggs. Marion had been "the perfect spy o' the time" in taking them from the pot, but then she would as usual have her husband eat them, and he as usual declared he neither needed nor wanted them. This night, however, he did not insist, but at once proceeded to prepare one, with which, as soon as it was nicely mixed with salt, he began to feed to Steenie. The boy had been used to being fed thus more than most children, and having taken the first mouthful instinctively, now moved his head so that his father might feed him more comfortably. He took every spoonful given him, and so ate both eggs, greatly to the delight of the rest of the company.

A moment more and Steenie got up. His father rose also.

"I'll convoy ye a bit, my man," he said.

"Eh, na! Ye needna that, father! It's near-hand yer bedtime! I'll jist be aboot i' the night—maybe a stane's cast from the door, maybe the ither side o' the Horn. Here or there I'm never far. I think whiles I'm jist like one o' them that ye call dead—I'm no away. I'm aboot somewhere!"

So saying, he went. He never on any occasion wished them good-night. That would be to leave them, and he was not leaving them. He was with them all the time!

CHAPTER EIGHT

David and His Daughter

The instant Steenie was gone, Kirsty went a step or two nearer to her father, and, looking up in his face, said, "I saw Francie Gordon the day, father."

"Weel, lassie, I reckon that wasna any strange occurrence! Where saw ye him?"

"He came to me o' the Hornside, where I sat weavin my stocking, over the bog on his powny—a right bonny thing and clever—a new one he's gotten from his mither. And it's no the first time he's been over there to see me since he came home!"

"Whatfor goes he there? That wasna the best o' places to go ridin' in!"

"He kenned where he was likest to see me. It was me he wanted."

"He wanted you, did he? And he's been more nor once after ye? Whatfor didna ye tell me afore, Kirsty?"

"We were bairns thegither, ye ken, father, and I never once thought the thing worth tellin ye aboot till the day. We've always been used to Francie comin and goin! I always looked at him as I would a bairn till the day. He spake straight oot the day, and I did the same and angered him."

"And whatfor are ye tellin me noo?"

" 'Cause it came intil my head that maybe it would be better—

no that it makes any differ I can see."

During this conversation Marion was washing the supper things, putting them away, and making general preparation for bed. She heard every word, and went about her work softly that she might hear, never opening her mouth to speak.

"There's somethin ye want to tell me and dinna like, lassie!" said David. "If ye be feared at yer father, go til yer mither. Fathers must sometimes be fearsome to lass-bairns!"

"Feared at my father? Na, na!" returned Kirsty, with a solemn face, looking straight into her father's eyes.

"Then it'll never be, or I must have a heap to blame myself for. I think if bairns kenned the terrible blame their fathers might have to endure for no doin better wi' them, they would be more particular to hold straight. I have been over muckle taken up wi' my beasts and my crops—more, God forgive me! Nor wi' my twa bairns. But He kens ye're more to me, the two, than ought else save the mither o' ye!"

"The beasts and the crops couldna weel do wi' less, and there was always our mither to see after us!"

"That's true, lassie! I only hope it wasna greed at the heart o' me! At the same time, who would I be greedy for but yerselves? Weel, and what's it all aboot? What made ye come to me aboot Francie? I'm some feared for him whiles, noo that he's so muckle oot o' our sight. The laddie's no by nature an ill laddie— far from 't! But it's a sore pity he couldna have been all his father's, and none o' him his mither's! But what's this aboot Francie?"

"Ow, father, nothin worth mentionin'! The daft loon would have had me promise to marry him—that's all!"

"The Lord preserve us!"

"There's no tellin what might have been i' the head o' him. He didna go so far as to say that anyway!"

"God forbid!" exclaimed her father with solemnity, after a short pause. "What said ye til him, lassie?"

"First I look at him—as weel as I can mind the nonsense o' 't— and called him the gowk he was. And he had the impudence to fall oot upo' me for carin more about Steenie nor the likes o' him!"

Her father looked very grave.

"Are you no pleased, father? I did what I thought right."

"Ye couldna have done better, Kirsty. But I'm sorry for the laddie, for, eh, but I loved his father! Lassie, for his father's sake I could take Francie intil the hoose, and work for him as for you and Steenie—though it's little guid Steenie ever gets o' me, poor soul!"

"Dinna say that, father. It would be an ill thing for Steenie to have anybody but yerself to the father o' him! A muckle part o' the night he wins over in lovin at you and his mother."

"And yerself, Kirsty."

"I'm thinkin I have my share i' the daytime."

"And hoo, think ye, goes the re~ o' the night wi' him?"

"The Bonny Man has the most o' 't, I dinna doobt, and what better could we desire for him! But, father, if Francie come back wi' the same tale—I dinna think he will after what I told him, but he may—what would ye have me say til him?"

"Say what ye will, lassie, so long as ye dinna let him for a moment believe there's a grain o' possibility i' the thing. Ye see, Kirsty,—"

"Ye dinna imagine, father, I could for one minute think otherwise aboot it nor ye do yerself! Don't I no ken that his father gave him in charge to you? And havena I therefore to look after him? Didna ye tell me all aboot yer grand friend, and hoo long ye had loved him? And didna that make Francie my business as weel's yer own? I'm verra sure his father would never approve o' any goins on atween him and a lassie sic like's myself, and fearna ye, father, but I shall hold him weel away. No that it's any struggle to me, though I always liked Francie! Havena I my own Steenie?"

"Gladly would I show Francie the road to sic a wife as ye would make him, my bonny Kirsty! But ye see clearly the thing itself's no to be thought upon. Eh, Kirsty, but it's grand to an old father's heart to hear ye take yer his part after sic a womanly fashion!"

"Am I no yer own lass-bairn, father? Where would I be wi' a

father that didna keep his word, and what less could I do nor help any man to keep his word? If breach o' the family word came through me, my life would go from me. But should I tell Francie's mither? I wouldna like to expose the folly o' him, but if ye think it guid, I'll go the morn's mornin'."

"I dinna think that would be weel. It would but raise a strife atween the twa, and do none an atom o' guid. She would only rage at the laddie, and put him in sic a red heat as would but weld thegither him and his will so that they would almost never come in twa again. And though ye went and told her yer own self, all the blame would be upon you none the less. There's no reason i' the puir body, and ye're nowise bound to her further nor to do right by her."

"I'm glad ye dinna want me to go," answered Kirsty. "She carries herself that grand that ye're almost driven to the consideration hoo little she's worth; and that's no the right spirit to have wi' any body or thing God thought worth makin."

CHAPTER NINE

At Castle Weelset

Francie's anger had died down a good deal by the time he reached home. He was, as his father's friend had just said, by no means a bad sort of fellow, only he was full of himself, and therefore of little use to anybody. His mother and he, when not actually at strife, were constantly on the edge of a quarrel. The two must each have their own way. Francie's way was sometimes good, his mother's sometimes not bad, but both were usually selfish. The boy had fits of generosity, the woman never, except toward her son. If she thought of something to please him, good and well! If he wanted anything of her, it would never do—the idea must be her own! If she imagined her son desired a thing, she felt she could not grant it, and told him so. Francis would not rest until he had exhausted the thing. Sudden division and high words would follow, with speechlessness on the mother's part which might last for days. All at once she would tire of it, and would appear at breakfast in the morning, looking as if nothing had ever come between them, and they would be the best of friends again for a few days, or perhaps a week. Then some fresh discord, no different in character from the preceding, would arise between them, and the same weary round be tramped again, each always in the right, and the other in the wrong. Every time they made it up, their relation seemed unimpaired, but it was hardly possible things should go on thus and not at length quite estrange their hearts.

In matters of display, to which Francis had much tendency, his mother's own vanity led her to indulge and spoil him, for she was always pleased he should look his best. On his real self she neither had nor sought any influence. Insubordination or arrogance in him actually pleased her. She liked him to show his spirit. Was it not a mark of his breeding?

Castle Weelset was not much of a castle. To an ancient, drafty, round tower had been added in the last century a rather large, defensible house. It stood on the edge of a gorge, crowning one of its stony hills of no great height. With scarce a tree to shelter it, the situation was very cold in winter, and it required a hardy breed to live there in comfort. There was little of a garden, and the stables were somewhat ruinous. For the former fact the climate sufficiently accounted, and for the latter, a long period of comparative poverty.

The young laird did not like farming, and had no love for books. In this interval between school and college, he found very little to occupy him, and even less to amuse him. Had Kirsty and her family proved as encouraging as he had expected, he would have made use of his new pony to ride to Corbyknowe in the morning and back to the castle at night.

His mother knew Old Barclay, as she called him, but had never shown him any cordiality. To treat him like a gentleman, even when he sat at her own table, she would have counted absurd. He had never been to the castle since the day after her husband's funeral, when she received him with such emphasized superiority that he felt he could not go again without running the risk either of having his influence with the boy ruined, or giving occasion to take Francis' part against his mother. Thereafter, he contented himself with making Francis welcome, and doing what he could to make the boy's visits pleasant. Francis delighted in drawing from his father's friend what tales he had to tell about their adventures together. In this way David's wife and children heard many things about David himself which would not otherwise have reached them. Naturally, Kirsty and

Francie grew to be good friends, and after they went to the parish school, there were few days indeed on which they did not walk at least as far home together as the midway divergence of their roads permitted. It was not unreasonable, therefore, that Francis should be, or should fancy himself, in love with Kirsty.

But all the time he thought of marrying her as a heroic deed, in raising the girl his mother despised to the lofty position he and that foolish mother imagined him to occupy. The anticipation of opposition from his mother naturally strengthened his determination. But he had never dreamed of opposition on the part of Kirsty. He assumed that the moment he stated his intention, she would be charmed, her mother more than pleased, and the stern old soldier overwhelmed with the honor of alliance with the son of his colonel. However, he did have an affection for Kirsty far deeper and better than his notion of their relations to each other would indicate. Although it was mainly his pride that suffered in his humiliating dismissal, he had a genuine heartache as he galloped home. When he reached the castle, he left his pony to go where he would, and rushed to his room. There, locking the door that his mother might not enter, he threw himself on his bed in the luxurious consciousness of a much-wronged lover. An uneducated country girl, for as such he regarded her, had cast from her, and not without insult, his splendidly generous offer of himself!

But poor rejected Francis did not shed many tears for the loss of his farm maiden. By and by he forgot everything, found he had gone to sleep and, endeavoring to weep again, did not succeed.

He grew hungry soon, and went down to see what was to be had. It was long past the usual hour for dinner, but Mrs. Gordon had not seen him return, and had had it put back, so to make the most of an opportunity of a quarrel. Nevertheless, she let it slide.

"Gracious, you've been crying!" she exclaimed, the moment she saw him.

Now certainly Francis had not cried much, but his eyes were a little red. He had not yet learned to lie, but he might then have made his first assay had he had a fib at his tongue's end. As he had not, he gloomed deeper, and made no answer.

"You've been fighting!" said his mother.

"Na, I haven," he returned with rude indignation. "If I had been, do ye think I would have cried?"

"You forget yourself, laird!" remarked Mrs. Gordon, more annoyed with his Scotch than the tone of it. "I would have you remember I am mistress of the house!"

"Till I marry, mother!" rejoined her son.

"Oblige me in the meantime," she answered, "by leaving vulgar accents outside it."

Francis was silent, and his mother, content with her victory, and in her own untruthfulness of nature believing he had indeed been fighting and had had the worst of it, said no more, but began to pity and pet him. A pot of his favorite jam presently consoled him—in the acceptance of which consolation he showed himself far less unworthy than many a grown man, similarly circumstanced, in the choice of his.

CHAPTER TEN

David and Francis

One day there was a market at a town some eight or nine miles off, and for lack of anything else to do, Francis had gone to display himself and his pony, which he was riding with so tight a curb that the poor thing every now and then reared in protest against the agony he suffered.

On one of these occasions Don was on the point of falling backward, when a brown wrinkled hand laid hold of him by the head, half pulling the reins from his rider's hand, and before he had quite settled again on his forelegs, had unhooked the chain of his curb, and fastened it some three links looser. Francis was more than indignant, even when he saw that the hand was Mr. Barclay's. Was he to be treated as one who did not know what he was about?

"Hoots, my man," said David gently, "there's no occasion to put a water-chain upo' the bonny beastie. He has a mouth like a leddy's, and to have 't linked up so tight is nothin less nor torture til him! It's a wonder to me he hasna broken yer bones and his own back thegither, poor thing!" he added, patting and stroking the spirited little creature that stood sweating and trembling.

"I thank you, Mr. Barclay," said Francis insolently, "but I am quite able to manage the brute myself. You seem to take me for a fool!"

" 'Deed, he's no so far off one that could call a bonny creature like that a brute!" returned David, nowise pleased to discover such hardness in one whom he would gladly treat like a child of his own. It was a great disappointment to him to see the lad getting further away from the possibility of being helped by him. "What would yer father say to see ye ill use any helpless bein'! Yer father was awful guid til 'is horse fowk!" The last word was one of David's own. He was a great lover of animals.

"I'll do with my own as I please!" cried Francis, and spurred the pony to pass David. But one stalwart hand held the pony fast, while the other seized his rider by the ankle. The old man was now thoroughly angry with the graceless youth.

"God bless my soul!" he cried. "Have ye the spurs on as weel? Stick one o' them intil him again and I'll cast ye from the saddle. I' the thick o' a fight, the long blades playin aboot yer father's head like lights i' the north, he never spurred his charger needless!"

"I don't see," said Francis, who had begun to cool down a little, "how he could have enjoyed the fight much if he never forgot himself! I should forget everything in the delight of the battle!"

"Yer father, laddie, never forgot anythin *but* himself. Forgettin himself left him free to mind anythin besides. Ye would forget everythin but yer own rage! Yer father was a great man as weel as a great solger, Francie, and a deevil to fight, as his men said. I have myself seen by the set mouth that the teeth were clinched i' the inside o' 't, when all the time on the surface o' him sat never a runkle. If ever there was a man that could think o' twa things at once, yer father could think o' three; and the three were God, his enemy, and the beast aneath him. Francie, Francie, i' the name o' yer father, I beg ye to regard the rights o' the neighbor ye sit upo'. If ye dinna that, ye'll come or long to think little o' yer human neighbor as weel, carin only for what ye get oot o' him!"

A voice inside Francis took part with the old man, and made him yet angrier. Also his pride was annoyed that his tenant should, in the hearing of two or three loafers gathered behind him, of whose presence the old man was unaware, not only rebuke him but address him by his name and the diminutive of it. So when David, in the appeal that burst from his enthusiastic remembrance of his officer in the battlefield, let the pony's head go, Francis dug his spurs in his sides, and darted off like an arrow. The old man stared openmouthed after him. The fools around laughed. David turned and walked away, his head sunk on his breast.

Francis had not ridden far before he was vexed with himself. He was not so much sorry, as annoyed that he had behaved in fashion undignified. The thought that his childish behavior would justify Kirsty in her opinion of him, added its sting. He tried to console himself with the reflection that this sort of thing ought to be put an end to at once. Otherwise, how far might not the old fellow's interference go! He even said to himself that such was a consequence of familiarity with inferiors. Yet angry as he was at his faultfinding, he would have been proud of any approval from the lips of the old soldier. He rode his pony mercilessly for a mile or so, then pulled up and began to talk pettingly to him, which Don did not find consoling, for only love makes petting worth anything, and the love here was not much to the front.

About halfway home, he had to ford a small stream, or go round two miles by a bridge. There had been much rain in the night, and the stream was considerably swollen. As he approached the ford, he met a knife grinder who warned him not to attempt it—he said he had nearly lost his wheel in it. But Francis always found it hard to accept advice. His mother had so often predicted evils which never followed, that he had come to think counsel the one thing not to be heeded.

"Thank you," he said. "I think we can manage it," and rode on.

When he reached the ford, where of all places he ought to have left the pony's head free, he foolishly remembered the curb-chain, and getting off, took it up a couple of links.

But when he remounted, whether from dread of the rush of

the brown water, or resentment at the threat of renewed torture, the pony would not take the ford, and a battle arose between them in which Francis was so far victorious that, after many attempts to run away, little Don, rendered desperate by the spur, dashed wildly into the stream and went plunging on for two or three yards. Then he fell, and Francis found himself rolling in the water, swept along by the current.

A little way lower down, at a sharp turn of the stream under a high bank, was a deep pool, a place held much in dread by the country lads and lasses, being a haunt of the kelpie. Francis knew the spot well, and had good reason to fear that, carried into it, he must be drowned, for he could not swim. Roused by the thought to a yet harder struggle, he succeeded in getting upon his feet; and reaching the bank exhausted, he lay there for a while. When at length he came to himself and rose, he found the water still between him and home, and nothing of his pony to be seen. If the youth's good sense had been equal to his courage, he would have been a fine fellow; he dashed straight into the ford, floundered through it, and lost his footing no more than Don would have, treated properly. When he reached the high ground on the other side, he could still see nothing of him, and with sad heart concluded him carried into the kelpie's hole, never more to be seen alive. What would his mother and Mr. Barclay say? Shivering and wretched, and with a growing compunction in regard to his behavior to Don, he crawled wearily home.

Don, however, had at no moment been in much danger. Rid of his master, he could take very good care of himself. He got to the bank without difficulty, and took care it should be on the homeside of the stream. Not once looking behind him after his tyrant, he set off at a good round trot, much refreshed by his bath, and rejoicing in the thought of his loose box at Castle Weelset.

In a narrow part of the road, however, he overtook a cart of Mr. Barclay's and, as he attempted to pass between it and the steep brae, the man on the shaft caught at his bridle, made him prisoner, tied him to the cart behind, and took him to

Corbyknowe. When David came home and saw him, he conjectured pretty nearly what had happened, and tired as he was, set out for the castle. Had he not feared that Francis might have been injured, he would not have cared to go, much as he knew it must relieve him to learn that his pony was safe.

Mrs. Gordon declined to see David, but he ascertained from the servants that Francis had come home half drowned, leaving Don in the kelpie's hole.

David hesitated a little whether or not to punish him for his behavior to the pony by allowing him to remain in ignorance of his safety, and so leaving him to his conscience. But concluding that such was not his part, he told them that the animal was safe at Corbyknowe, and went home again.

But he wanted Francis to fetch the pony himself, therefore did not send him, and in the meantime fed and groomed him with his own hands as if he had been his friend's charger. Francis had just enough of the grace of shame to make him shrink from going go Corbyknowe. So his mother wrote to David, asking why he did not send home the animal. The courteous David would take no order from any but his superior officer, and answered that he would gladly give Don up to the young laird in person.

The next day Mrs. Gordon drove to Corbyknowe. Arrived there, she declined to leave her carriage, requesting Mrs. Barclay, who came to the door, to send her husband to her. Mrs. Barclay thought it better to comply.

David came in his shirt sleeves, for he had been fetched from his work.

"If I understand your answer to my request, Mr. Barclay, you decline to send back Mr. Gordon's pony. Pray, on what grounds?"

"I wrote, ma'am, that I should be glad to give him over to Mr. Francis himself."

"Mr. Gordon does not find it convenient to come all this way on foot. In fact he declines to do it, and requests that you send the pony home this afternoon."

"Excuse me, ma'am, but it's surely enough done that a man

make known the presence o' strays, and take proper care o' them until they're claimed! I was fain to give the bonny thing a bit o' pleasure in life. Francie's over hard upo' him."

"You forget, Mr. Barclay, that Mr. Gordon is your landlord!"

"His father, ma'am, was my landlord, and his father's father was my father's landlord, and the interests o' the landlord have always been oors!"

"You presume on my late husband's kindness to you, Barclay!"

"If devotion be presumption, ma'am, I presume. Archibald Gordon was and is my friend, and will be forever. We have been through muckle thegither to change to one anither. It was for his sake and the laddie's own that I wanted him to come to me. I wanted a word wi' him aboot that pony o' his. He'll never be a true man that takes no care o' dumb animals! You that's so weel at home in the saddle yerself, ma'am, might take a kindly care o' what's aneath his!"

"I will have no one interfere with my son. I am quite capable of teaching him his duty myself."

"His father requested me to do what I could for him, ma'am."

"His *late* father, if you please, Barclay!"

"He shall never be Francie's *late* father to Francie, if I can help it, ma'am! He may be your *late* husband, ma'am, but he's my cornel yet, and I shall keep my word til him! It'll no be long noo, i' the nature o' things, till I go til him, and sure am I his first word'll be aboot the laddie. I would ill like to answer him, 'Archie, I ken nothin aboot him but what I could weel wish itherwise!' Hoo would ye like to give sic an answer yerself, ma'am?"

"I'm surprised at a man of your sense, Barclay, thinking we shall know one another in heaven! We shall have to be content with God there!"

"I said nothin about heaven, ma'am! Fowk may ken one anither and no be in one place. I took note i' the kirk last Sunday that Abraham kenned the rich man, and the rich man him, and they warna i' the same place. But ye'll let the yoong laird come and see me, ma'am?" concluded David, changing his tone and speaking as one who begged a favor; for the thought of meeting his old friend and having nothing to tell him about his boy, quenched his pride.

"Home, Thomas!" cried her late husband's wife to her coachman, and drove away.

"They'll have to give that wife a hell til herself!" said David, turning to the door discomfited.

"And maybe she'll no like it when she has 't!" returned his wife, who had heard every word. "There's fowk that's no fit company for anybody, and I'm thinkin she's one if there no be anither!"

"I'll send the powny the night," said David. "A body canna insist where fowk are no friends. That would grow to enmity, and the end o' all guid. Na, we must send home the powny, and if there be any grace i' the bairn, he canna but come and say thank-ye!"

Mrs. Gordon rejoiced in her victory, but David's yielding showed itself the true policy. Francis did call and thank him for taking care of Don. He even granted that perhaps he had been too hard on the pony.

"Ye could righteously expect nothin o' a powny o' his size that that powny o' yours couldna do, Francie!" said David. "But i' God's name, dear laddie, be a righteous man. If ye require no more than's fair from man or beast, ye'll mostly aye get it. But if yer ootlook in life be to get anythin and give nothin, ye must come to grief. Success in an ill attempt is the worst failure a man can make."

But it was talking to the wind, for Francis thought that David, like his mother, was bent on finding fault with him. He made haste to get away, and left his friend with a sad heart.

He rode on to the foot of the Horn, to the spot where Kirsty was usually at that season to be found; but she saw him coming and went up the hill. Soon after, his mother contrived that he should pay a visit to some relatives in the south, and for a time neither the castle nor the Horn saw anything of him. Without returning home he went in the winter to Edinburgh, where he neither disgraced nor distinguished himself. David was glad to hear no ill of him. To be beyond his mother's immediate influence was perhaps to his advantage; but as nothing superior was substituted, it was at best but little gain. His companions were like himself, such as might turn to worse or better, no one could tell which.

CHAPTER ELEVEN

Kirsty and Phemy

During the first winter Francis spent at college, his mother was in England, and remained there all the next summer and winter. When she came home, she was even less pleasant than before in the eyes of her household, no one of which had ever loved her. Throughout the summer she had a succession of visitors, and stories began to spread concerning strange doings at the castle. The neighbors talked of extravagance, and the censorious among them of riotous living; while Donal, the butler, more than hinted that the amount of wine and whiskey consumed was far in excess of the amount served when the old colonel was alive.

One of them, who acted as housekeeper, had known David Barclay from his boyhood, and understood his real intimacy with her late master. She would open her mind to him, while keeping silent toward everyone else concerning her mistress' affairs. None of the stories current in the countryside came from her. David was to Mrs. Bremner the other side of a deep pit, into the bottom of which whatever was said between them dropped.

"There'll come a catastroff afore long," said Mrs. Bremner one evening when David Barclay overtook her on the road to the town, "and that'll be seen! The property's jist goin to the dogs! There's Maister Donal, goin aboot like one in a dilemm as to cuttin 'is throat! He darena say a word, ye see! The old laird trusted him, and he's feared that he be blamed, but there's no doin anythin wi' that woman. The siller must be forthcomin when she's wantin it!"

"The siller's no hers any more nor the land; it's the yoong laird's!" remarked David.

"That's true, but she's i' the power o' 't till he come o' age, and Maister Donal, poor man, many's the time he's jist driven to get what's aye wanted! What comes o' the siller it jist sickens me to think. I'm not doobtin the drink's gettin a sore grip o' her!"

"Deed I wouldna be surprised!" returned David. "Eh, to think o' Archie Gordon takin til himself sic a wife! That a man like him, o' good report, and come to years o' descretion—to think o' brains like his turnin as fozy as an auld neep at sight o' a bonny woman!"

"Bonny, David! Called ye the mistress bonny?"

"She used to be—bonny, that is, as a button or a buckle might be bonny. What she may be the now, I havena set eye upon her since she came to the Knowe orderin me to send back Francie's powny. If she has a spot o' beauty left, the drink'll take it or it have done wi' her!"

"Or she have done wi' 't, David! It's taken the color from her a'ready, and begun to give her anither! But it concerns me more aboot Francie; what's to come o' him when all's gone? What'll there be for him to come intil?"

Gladly would David have interfered, but he was helpless; he had no legal guardianship over the boy! Nothing could be done till he was a man, "if he ever be a man!" said David to himself with a sigh, and thought how much better off he was with his half-witted Steenie than his friend with his clever Francie.

Mrs. Bremner was sister-in-law to the schoolmaster, and was then on her way to see him and his daughter, Phemy. From childhood the girl had been in the way of going to the castle to see her aunt, and was well known about the place. Being an engaging child, she had become not only welcome to the servants but something of a favorite with the mistress, whom she amused with her little airs and pleased with her winning manners. She was now about fourteen, a half-blown beauty. She had long been a vain little thing, approving of her own looks in the glass, and taking much interest in setting them off, but so simple as to make no attempt at concealing her self-satisfaction. Her pleased contemplation of this or that portion of her person, and the frantic attempts she was sometimes seen making to get sight of her back, especially when she was wearing a new frock, were indeed more amusing than hopeful, but her vanity was not yet so pronounced as to overshadow her better qualities. Kirsty had not thought it well to take notice of it, but she was already a little anxious about Phemy's obsession with dress and appearance, especially since her aunt, like her father, neither saw nor imagined fault in her.

That the child had no mother drew her to Kirsty, whose mother was her strength and joy, while gratitude to the child's father, who, in opening for her some doors of wisdom and more of knowledge, had put her under eternal obligations, moved her to make what return she could. It deepened her sense of debt to Phemy that the schoolmaster did not do for his daughter anything like what he had for years been doing for his pupil; Kirsty almost felt as if she had diverted to her own use much that rightly belonged to Phemy. At the same time she knew very well that had she never existed, the relation between the father and the daughter would have been the same. Seeing the child of his dearly loved wife, the schoolmaster was utterly content with his Phemy. He felt as if she knew everything her mother knew, had the same inward laws of being and the same disposition, and was simply, like her, perfect.

That she should ever do anything wrong was an idea inconceivable to him. Nor was there much chance of his discovering it if she did. When not at work, he was constantly reading. Where most people close a book without having gained from it a single germ of thought, Mr. Craig seldom opened one without falling directly into a brown study over something suggested by it. Like many Scots, while Phemy was his one joy, he seldom showed her sign of affection, seldom made her feel, and never sought to make her feel how he loved her.

That his child required to be taught had scarcely occurred to the man who could not have lived without teaching—as witness the eagerness with which he would help Kirsty along any path of knowledge in which he knew how to walk. The love of knowledge had grown in him to a possessing passion, paralyzing in a measure those powers of his life sacred to life—that is, to God and his neighbor.

Kirsty could not do nearly what she would to make up for his neglect. For one thing, the child did not take to learning, and though she loved Kirsty and often tried to please her, she would not keep on doing anything without being more frequently reminded of her duty than the distance between their two abodes permitted. Kirsty had her to the farm as often as the schoolmaster would consent to her absence, and kept her as long as he kept on forgetting it. Phemy was always glad to go to Corbyknowe, and always glad to get away again. For Mrs. Barclay thought it her part to teach her household manners, and lessons of that sort Phemy relished worse than some of a more intellectual nature. If left with Mrs. Barclay, the moment Kirsty appeared again, the child would fling from her whatever might be in her hand, and flee as to her deliverer from bondage and hard labor. Then Kirsty would always insist on her finishing what she had been at, and Phemy would obey, with the protest of silent tears and the airs of a much injured mortal. Had Kirsty been backed by the child's father, she might have made something of her; but it grew more and more painful to think of her future, when her self-constituted guardian should have lost what influence she had over her.

Phemy was rather afraid of Steenie. Her sunny nature shrank from the shadow, as of a wall, in which Steenie appeared to her always to stand. Although never rude to him, she would involuntarily recoil from any little attention he would offer her, and he soon learned to leave her undismayed. Though he never spoke of it, Kirsty saw quite plainly that the child's repugnance troubled him, for she could read his face like a book, and heard him sigh when even his mother did not. Her eyes were constantly regarding him, like sheep feeding on the pasture of his face.

The thoughts that strayed over his face were the sheep to which all her life she had been the devoted shepherdess.

At Corbyknowe things went on as before. Kirsty was in no danger of tiring of the even flow of her life. Steenie's unselfish solitude of soul made him every day dearer to her. She had no thought of distinguishing herself, no smallest ambition of becoming learned. Her soul was thirsty to understand, and what she understood found its way from her mind into her life. Much to the advantage of her thinking were her keen power and constant practice of observation. We can do and think without words, but certainly the more forms we have ready to embody our thoughts, the further we shall be able to carry our thinking. Richly endowed, Kirsty required the more mental food, and was the more able to use it when she found it. To such of the neighbors as had no knowledge of any diligence save that of the hands, she seemed to lead an idle life, but, indeed, Kirsty's hands were far from idle. When not with Steenie she was almost always at the call of her mother who, from the fear that she might grow up incapable of managing a house, often required a good deal of her. But the mother did not fail to note with what alacrity she would lay her book aside, sometimes even dropping it in her eagerness to answer her summons. Then, dismissed for the moment, she would at once take her book again, and the seat nearest to it. She could read anywhere, and gave herself none of the student airs that make some young people so pitifully unpleasant. Because solitude was preferable for study, Kirsty was always glad to find herself with her books in the little hut, Steenie asleep on the heather carpet on her feet, and with the assurance that no one would interrupt her.

In the sweet absence of selfish cares, her mind full of worthy thoughts, and her heart going out in tenderness, it was only natural that Kirsty's face shoud go on growing in beauty and refinement. She had not yet arrived at physical full growth, and the forms of her person being therefore in a process of change were the more easily modeled after her spiritual nature. She seemed almost already one who would not die, but live forever and continue to inherit the earth. Neither her father nor her mother could have imagined anything better to be made of her.

Steenie had not changed his habits, neither seemed he to grow at all more like other people. He was now seldom so much depressed as formerly, but he showed no sign of less dependence on Kirsty.

CHAPTER TWELVE

The Earthhouse

About a year after Francis Gordon went to Edinburgh, Kirsty and Steenie made a discovery.

Between Corbyknowe and the Horn, on whose sides David Barclay had a right of pasturage for the few sheep to which Steenie and Snootie were the shepherds, was a small glen. Through it, on its way to join the little river with the kelpie-pot, ran a brook with nice grassy banks. The brother and sister always crossed this brook when they wanted to go straight to the top of the hill.

One morning, having each taken the necessary run and jump, they had begun to climb on the other side when Kirsty, who was a few paces before him, turned at an exclamation from Steenie.

"It's all the weight o' my feet!" he cried, as he dragged one of the troublesome members out of a hole. "Losh, I dinna ken hoo far it might have gone doon if I hadna gotten a hold o' 't in time and pulled it oot!"

How much of humor, silliness, and truth were wrapped up together in some of the things he said was impossible to determine. Kirsty came pretty near knowing, but even she was not always sure where willful oddity and where misapprehension was at the root of a remark.

"But there was no hole!" continued Steenie. "There couldna

have been. There's the hole noo! My foot made it. Luik ye there! Ye see the twa stanes standin up by themselves, and there's the hole atween the twa! There couldna have been a hole there afore the weight o' my feet came doon upo' the spot! I went in a'most til my knee!"

"Let's luik!" said Kirsty, and proceeded to examine the place.

She thought at first it must be the burrow of some animal, but the similarity in shape of the projecting stones suggested that their position might not be fortuitous. She looked a little closer, pulling away the heather about the mouth of the opening, and Steenie set himself to help her. Kirsty was stronger than Steenie, but he always did his best to help her in anything that required exertion.

They soon spied the lump of sod and heather which Steenie's heavy foot had driven down, and when they had pulled that out, they saw that the hole went deeper still. Having widened the mouth of it by clearing away a thick growth of roots from one of its sides, and taken out a quantity of soft earth, they could tell that it went sloping into the ground still farther. With growing curiosity they leaned down into it, lying on the edge, and reaching with their hands removed the loose earth as low as they could. This done, the descent showed itself about two feet square, as far down as they had cleared it, beyond which a little way it was lost in the dark.

There was yet greater inducement to go on, but Kirsty knew Steenie had a horror of dark places, associating them somehow with the grave. There might be some animal inside. Steenie thought not, for there was no opening until he made it! Kirsty thought not, because she knew no wild animal in the region larger than fox or badger, neither of which would have made such a big hole. But then her imagination was nearly too much for her! What if some huge bear had been asleep in it for hundreds of years, and growing all the time! Certainly he could not get out, but if she roused him, and he got a hold of her. . . . The next instant her courage revived for she would have been ashamed to let what she did not believe influence any action. The passage must lead somewhere, and it was large enough for her to explore it!

Telling Steenie that if he heard her cry out, he must get hold of her feet and pull, she laid herself on the ground and crept in head first—in which lay the advantage that she would meet any danger face to face! She thought it must lead to an ancient tomb, but said nothing of the conjecture for fear of horrifying Steenie who stood trembling, sustained only by his faith in Kirsty.

She went down and down and quite disappeared—not a foot was left for Steenie to lay hold of. Terrible and long seemed the time to him as he stood there forsaken, Kirsty out of sight in the heart of the earth. He knew there were wolves in Scotland once; who could tell but that a she-wolf had been left, and a whole clan of them lived there underground, never issuing in the daytime! What if one of them got Kirsty by the throat before she had time to cry out! Then he thought she might have gone till she could go no farther, and not having room to turn, was trying to creep backward, but her clothes hindered her. Forgetting his repugnance in overmastering fear, the faithful fellow was already half inside the hole to go after her, when up shot Kirsty's head almost in his face. For a moment he was terribly perplexed. He had been expecting her feet, not her head: how could she have gone in head first, and not come back feet first?

"Eh, Kirsty," he said in a fearstruck whisper, "it's awful to see ye come oot like a worm!"

"Ye saw me go in, Steenie, ye gowk!" returned Kirsty, dismayed at sight of his solemn dread.

"Ay," answered Steenie, "but I didna see ye come oot! Eh, Kirsty, have ye a head at both ends o' ye?"

Kirsty's laughter blew Steenie's discomposure away, and he too laughed.

"Come back hame," said Kirsty. "I must get hold o' a candle! Yon place must be seen intil. I never saw, or rather felt, the like o' 't. There's room enough—ye can see that wi' yer arms!"

"What is there room enough for?" asked Steenie.

"For you and me, and twenty or thirty more, mebbe—I dinna ken," replied Kirsty.

"I should make ye a present o' my room," returned Steenie. "I want none o' 't."

"I'll go doon wi' the candle," said Kirsty, "and see whether 't be a place for ye. If I cry oot, 'Ay is 't,' will ye come?"

"That I will, if 'twere the whale's belly!" relied Steenie.

They set off for the house, talking as they walked.

"I won'er what the place could ever have been for!" said Kirsty, more to herself than Steenie. "It's bigger nor any thought I had o' 't."

"What is 't like, Kirsty?" inquired Steenie.

"Hoo can I tell when I saw nothin!" replied Kirsty. "But," she added thoughtfully, "if it werena that we're in Scotland but were nigh t' Rome, I would have been a'most sure I was in one o' the catacombs!"

"Eh, losh, let me away to the hill!" cried Steenie, stopping and half turning. "I canna bide the verra word o' the creatures!"

"What creatures?" asked Kirsty, a little surprised.

"To think," he went on, "o' a whole kirk o' cats aneath the earth! Kirsty, ye willna think it a place for *me*? Ye see I'm no like ither fowk, and sic a thing might drive me oot o' all the small wits ever I had!"

"Hoots!" rejoined Kirsty with a smile. "The catacombs had nothing to do wi' cats!"

"Tell me what are they, then."

"The catacombs," answered Kirsty, "was what in auld times, and no i' this country even, they called the places where they laid their dead."

"Eh, Kirsty, but that's worse!" returned Steenie. "I wouldna go intil sic a place—na, no for what the warld could give me! No for long Lowrie's fiddle and all the tunes in 't! I would never get my feet o' 't! They'd hold me there!"

Then Kirsty began to tell him, as she would have taught a child, something of the history of the catacombs, knowing how it would interest him.

"I' the days langsyne," she said, "there was fowk, like you and me, that loved the Bonny Man. The verra sound o' His name was enough to make their hearts full wi' doonright gladness. And they went here and there and all aboot, and told everybody aboot Him. Fowk that didna ken Him, and didna want to ken Him, couldna bide to hear tell o' Him, and they said, 'Let's have no more o' this! Have done wi' yer Bonny Man! Hold yer tongues.' But the others wouldna hear o' holdin their tongues. A body must ken aboot Him! 'So long's we have tongues, and can wag them to the name o' Him,' they said, 'we'll no hold them!' And at that they fell upo' them, and ill-used them sore. Some o' them they took and burnt alive, and some o' them they flung to the wild beasts. But the puir fowk said the Bonny Man was wi' them! They didna care!"

"Ay, of course," interrupted Steenie. "If He was wi' them they wouldna mind a hair, or at least no twa hairs! Who would! If He be in yon hole, Kirsty, I'll go back and crawl intil 't. I will now!" And he turned and had run some distance before Kirsty succeeded in stopping him.

"Steenie! Steenie!" she cried. "I dinna doobt He's there, for He's ever'where, but ye ken yerself ye canna always see Him, and maybe ye wouldna see Him there now, and might think He wasna there. Bide till we have a light, and I'll go doon first."

Steenie was persuaded, and turned and came back to her. To father, mother, and sister he was always obedient, even on the rare occasions when it cost him much to be so.

"Ye see, Steenie," she continued, "I dinna ken yet what yon place is. I was only goin to tell ye aboot the places it reminded me o'! Would ye like to hear aboot them?"

"I would that, right weel! Say away, Kirsty."

"The fowk that loved the Bonny Man gathered themselves always thegither to have talks wi' one anither aboot Him and, as I was tellin ye, the fowk that didna care aboot Him were angered, and set upo' them, and jist would have none o' them nor Him. So the fowk counseled thegither, and gathered in a place where nobody would think o' lookin for them—where but i' the bowels o' the earth, where they laid their dead away upo' shelfs!"

"Eh, but that was fearsome!" interposed Steenie. "They must have been sore set! If I had been there, would they have made me go wi' them?"

"Na, no if ye didna like. But ye would have liked 't. It wasna an ill way to bury fowk, nor an ill place to go til. I reckon it would be some hard kind o' rock, and when the dead was laid in 't, they closed it up—the mouth o' the shelf, that is—so each was weel closed in."

"But what for didna they bury their dead i' their kirkyards?"

" 'Cause theirs was a great muckle town, wi' sic a heap o' hooses that there wasna room for kirkyards. Outside o' town, there they had caves wi' a lot o' passages, and here and there a wee roomy like, wi' ither entrances goin from them this way and that. So, when they took themselves there, the friends o' the Bonny Man would fill one o' the roomies, and close in one o' the passages that went from 't, and that way, though there couldna many o' them see one anither at once, some would hear. They could speak loud oot, and a body ootside hear nothin and suspect nothin. And jist think, Steenie, there's a picture o' the Bonny Man Himself painted upo' the way o' one o' those places doon aneath the ground!"

As they drew near the house, their mother saw them coming, and went to the door to meet them.

"We're wantin a bit o' candle, mother," said Kirsty.

"What want ye a candle for i' the midst o' the daylight?" asked the mother.

"We want to go doon a hole," replied Steenie with flashing eyes, "and see the picture o' the Bonny Man."

"Hoot, Steenie! I telled ye it wasna there," interposed Kirsty.

"Na," returned Steenie, "ye only said yon hole wasna that place. Ye said the Bonny Man *was* there, though I mightna see Him. Ye didna say that picture wasna there."

"The picture's no there, Steenie. We've come upon a hole, mother, that we want to go doon intil and see what it's like," said Kirsty.

"Preserve us, lassie! Take care where ye carry the bairn!" cried the mother. "But, eh, take him where ye like," she substituted, correcting herself. "The laddie needs twa mithers, and the Merciful has given him the twa! Ye're more his mither nor me, Kirsty!"

She asked no more questions, but got them the candle and let them go. They hastened back, Steenie in his most jubilant mood, which always seemed to have in it a touch of deathly frost and a flash as of the primal fire. What could be the strange displacement or maladjustment which, in the brain harboring the immortal thing, troubled it so, and made it yearn after an untasted liberty? The source of his jubilance now was easy to tell: the idea of the Bonny Man was, in that troubled brain of his, associated with the place into which they were about to descend.

The moment they reached the spot, Kirsty, to the renewed astonishment of Steenie, dived at once into the ground, and disappeared.

"Kirsty! Kirsty!" he cried out after her, and danced like a terrified child. Then he shook with fresh dismay at the muffled sound that came back to him in answer from the unseen hollows of the earth.

Already Kirsty stood at the bottom of the sloping tunnel, and was lighting her candle. When it burned up, she found herself looking into a level gallery, the roof of which she could touch. It was not an excavation, but had been trenched from the surface, for it was roofed with great slabs of stone. Its sides, of rough stones, were six or seven feet apart at the floor paved with small boulders, but sloped so much toward each other that at the top their distance was less by about two and a half feet. Kirsty was a keen observer, and her power of seeing had been greatly developed through her constant conscientious endeavor to realize every description she read.

She went on about ten or twelve yards, and came to a bend in the gallery, another small chamber that branched into a second gallery, which soon came to an end. The place was not unlike a catacomb, only its two built galleries were much wider than the excavated thousands in the catacombs. She turned back to the entrance, left her candle there, and again startled Steenie, still staring into the mouth of the hole, with her sudden reappearance.

"Would ye like to come doon, Steenie?" she asked. "It's a strange place."

"Is 't awful fearsome?" asked Steenie, shrinking.

His feeling of dismay was not inconsistent with his pleasure in being out on the wild waste hillside, when heaven and earth were absolutely black, not seldom the whole of the night, in utter loneliness to eye or ear, and his never then feeling anything like dread. Then and there only did he seem to have room enough. His terror was of the smallest pressure on his soul, the least hint at imprisonment. That he could not rise and wander among the stars at his will, shaped itself to him as the heaviness of his feet holding him down.

"No a bit," answered Kirsty, who felt awe anywhere—on hilltop, in churchyard, in sunlit silent room—but never fear. "It's as like the place I was tellin ye aboot—"

"Ay, the cat place!" interrupted Steenie.

"The place wi' the picture," returned Kirsty.

Steenie darted forward, shot headfirst into the hole as he had seen Kirsty do, and crept undismayed to the bottom of the slope. Kirsty followed close behind, but he was already on his feet when she joined him. He grasped her arm eagerly, his face turned from her, and his eyes gazing fixedly into the depth of the gallery, lighted so vaguely by the candle on the floor of its entrance.

"I think I saw Him!" he said in a whisper full of awe and delight. "I think I did see Him! But Kirsty, hoo am I to be sure that I saw Him?"

"Maybe ye did and maybe ye didna see Him," replied Kirsty. "But that doesna matter so muckle, for He's always seein you, and ye'll see Him, and be sure that ye see Him, when the right time comes."

"I shall wait," answered Steenie confidently, and in silence followed Kirsty along the gallery.

This was Steenie's first, and all but his last, descent into the earthhouse, or *weem*, as a place of the sort is called. There are many such in Scotland, their age and origin objects of merest conjecture. The moment he was out of it, he fled to the Horn.

The next Sunday Steenie heard at church the story of the burial and resurrection of the Lord, and after their talk about the catacombs, associated the chamber they had just discovered with the tomb in which "they laid Him," at the same time concluding the top of the hill, where he had, as he believed, on certain favored nights met the Bonny Man, the place whence He ascended—to come again as Steenie thought He did! The earthhouse had no longer any attraction for Steenie; the Bonny Man was not there; He was risen! He was somewhere above the mountaintop haunted by Steenie, and that He sometimes descended upon it Steenie already knew, for had he not seen Him there?

Happy Steenie! Happier than so many Christians who, more in their brain-senses, but far less in their heart-senses than he, haunt the sepulchre as if the dead Jesus lay there still, and forget to walk the world with Him who dies no more, the Living One!

But his sister took a great liking to the place, nor was repelled by her mistaken suspicion that there the people of the land in times unknown had buried some of their dead. In the hot days, when the earthhouse was cool, and in winter when the thick blanket of snow lay over it and it felt warm as she entered it from the frosty wind, she would sit there in the dark, sometimes imagining herself one of the believers of old, thinking the Lord was at hand, approaching in person to fetch her and her friends. When the spring came, she carried down sod and turf and made for herself a seat in the central chamber, there to sit and think. By and by she fastened an oil lamp to the wall, and read by it. Occasionally she made a good peat fire, for she had found a chimney that went sloping into the upper air; and if it did not always draw well, peat smoke is as pleasant as wholesome, and she could bear a good deal of its smothering. Not unfrequently she carried her book there when no one was likely to want her, and enjoyed to the full the rare and delightful sense of absolute safety from interruption. Sometimes she would make a little song there, with which as she made it its own music would come, and she would model the air with her voice as she wrote the words in a little book on her knee.

CHAPTER THIRTEEN

A Visit from Francis Gordon

The summer following Francis Gordon's first session at college, Castle Weelset and Corbyknowe saw nothing of him. No one missed him much, and but for his father's sake no one would have thought much about him. Kirsty, as one who had told him the truth concerning himself, thought of him oftener than anyone except her father.

The summer after, Francis paid a short visit to Castle Weelset, and went one day to Corbyknowe, where he left a favorable impression upon all. The old imperiousness which made him so unlike his father had retired into the background; his smile, though not so sweet, came oftener, and his carriage was full of courtesy. But something was gone which his old friends would gladly have seen still. His behavior in the old time was not so pleasant, but he had been as one of the family. Often disagreeable, he was yet loving. Now, he laid himself out to make himself acceptable as a superior. Freed so long from his mother's lowering influences, what was of his father in him might by this time have come more to the surface but for certain ladies in Edinburgh, connections of the family who, influenced by his good looks and pleasant manners, and possibly by his position in the Gordon country, sought his favor by deeds of flattery, and succeeded in spoiling him not a little.

Steenie happened to be about the house when he came. Francie behaved to him so kindly that the gentle creature, overcome with grateful delight, begged him to go and see a house he and Kirsty were building.

In some families the games of the children mainly consist in the contruction of dwellings of this kind or that—castle, or ship, or cave, or nest in the treetop, according to the material attainable. It is an outcome of the aboriginal necessity for shelter, this instinct of burrowing. Steenie had very early shown it, probably from a vague consciousness of weakness, and Kirsty came heartily to his aid in following it, with the reaction of waking in herself a luxurious idea of sheltered safety. Northern children cherish in their imaginations the sense of protection more than others. This is partly owing to the severity of their climate, the snow and wind, the rain and sleet, the hail and darkness they encounter. An English child can never have such a sense of protection as a Scots bairn in bed on a winter night, his mother in the nursery, and the wind howling like a pack of wolves about the house.

Francis consented to go with Steenie to see his house, and Kirsty naturally accompanied them. By this time she had gathered the little that was known concerning *weems*, and as they went it occurred to her that it would be pleasant to the laird to be shown a thing on his own property of which he had never heard, and which, in the eyes of some, would add to its value. So Kirsty led the way past the weem.

She had so well cleared out its entrance, that it was now comparatively easy of access, else it was doubtful the young laird would have risked spoiling his admirably fitted clothes to satisfy the mild curiosity he felt regarding Kirsty's discovery. As it was, he pulled off his coat before entering, despite her assurance that he "needna fear spoilin anythin."

She went in before him to light her candle, and he followed. As she showed him the curious place, she gave him the results of her reading about such constructions, telling him who had written what. "There's more o' them, I gather," she said, "and more remarkable ones, in oor own county than in any other in

Scotland. I have myself seen none but this." Then she told him how Steenie had led the way to its discovery. By the time she ended, Francis was really interested—chiefly, no doubt, in finding himself possessor of a thing which many men, learned and unlearned, would think worth coming to see.

"Did you find this in it?" he asked, seating himself on her little throne of turf.

"Na, I put that there myself," answered Kirsty, "There was nothin in the place. There was nothin ye could have picked off o' the floor. If it hadna been oot o' the way o' the wind, ye would have thought it had swept it clean. Ye could have telled by nothin in 't whatever it was meant for, hoose or byre or barn, kirk or kirkyard. It had been jist a hidy-hole in troubled times, when the country would be swarmin wi' marauders!"

"What made ye the seat for, Kirsty?" asked Gordon, calling her by her name for the first time, and falling into the mother tongue with a flash of his old manner.

"I come here," she answered, "to be alone and read a bit. It's so quiet. Eternity seems itself to come and hide in 't. I'm tempted whiles to bide all night."

"Isna 't awfu' cold?"

"Na. It's fine and warm i' the winter. And I can light a fire when I like. But ye havena yer coat on, Francie! I oughtna to have let ye bide so long!"

He shivered, rose, and made his way out. Steenie stood in the sunlight waiting for them.

"Why, Steenie," said Gordon, "you brought me to see your house. Why didn't you come in with me?"

"This is no *my* hoose!" answered Steenie. "I'm buildin one, and Kirsty's helpin me. I couldna build a hoose wantin Kirsty! That's what I would have ye see, no this one. This is Kirsty's hoose. It was Kirsty wanted ye to see this one. Na, it's no mine," he added reflectively. "I ken I must come til 't some day, but I shall bide oot o' 't as long's I can. I like the hill a heap better."

"What *does* he mean?" asked Francis, turning to Kirsty.

"Ow, he has a heap o' notions o' 'is own!" answered Kirsty, who did not care to talk about her brother save to those who loved him.

When Francis turned again, he saw Steenie a good way up the hill.

"Where does he want to take me, Kirsty? Is it far?" he asked.

"Ay, it's a guid bitty—it's near the top o' the Horn."

"Then I think I shall not go," returned Francis. "I will come another day."

"Steenie! Steenie!" cried Kirsty, after the receding form of her brother. "He'll no go the day. He must go hame. He says he'll come anither time. Hold ye away on to yer hoose; I shall be wi' ye by and by."

Steenie went up the hill, and Kirsty and Francis walked toward Corbyknowe.

"Has no young man appeared yet to put Steenie's nose out of joint, Kirsty?" asked Gordon.

Kirsty thought the question rude, but answered with quiet dignity, "No one. I never had muckle opinion o' yoong men, and dinna care aboot their company. But what are ye thinkin o' doin yerself, I mean, when ye're through wi' the college?" she continued. "Ye'll surely be comin hame to take things intil yer own hand?"

"The property must look after itself, Kirsty. I will be a soldier like my father. If it could do without him when he was in India, it may just as well do without me. As long as my mother lives, she shall do as she likes with it."

Thus talking, and growing more friendly as they went, they walked slowly back to the house. There Francis mounted his horse and rode away, and for more than two years they saw nothing of him.

CHAPTER FOURTEEN

Steenie's House

Steenie seemed always to experience a strange sort of terror while waiting for anyone to come out of the weem, and his repugnance to the place was what chiefly moved him to build a house of his own. They still made use of their little hut as before, and Kirsty still kept her library there; but it was at the foot of the Horn, and Steenie loved the peak of the Horn more than any other spot in his narrow world.

After Steenie's only visit to the weem, he fled to the Horn, and there he roamed for hours, possessed with the feeling that he had all but lost Kirsty who had taken possession of a house into which he could never accompany her. For himself he would like a house on the very top of the Horn, not one inside it!

Near the top was a little scoop out of the hill, sheltered on all sides except the south. On one slope of the hollow, full in the face of the sun, a little family of oddly shaped rocks had fallen together. They were of stable equilibrium, with narrow spaces between them. The sun had been throwing his last red rays among these rocks one evening when Steenie wandered into the little valley. The moment his eye fell upon them, he said in his heart, "Yon's the place for a hoose! I'll get Kirsty to build one, and mebbe she'll come and bide in 't wi' me!"

For years Steenie had conflicting ideas of refuge in his mind.

One was embodied in the heathery hut with Kirsty, but for the last three years another had had the upper hand. It was typified by the uplifted loneliness, the air and space of the mountain upon which the Bonny Man sometimes descended. Now it seemed possible to have the two kinds of refuge together, where the more material would render the more spiritual easier to attain! These were not Steenie's words—indeed, he used none concerning the matter, but such were his vague feelings.

The spot had many advantages. For one thing, the group of rocks was the ready skeleton of the house Steenie wanted, and if the snow sometimes lay deeper there than on other parts of the hill, there first it began to melt. A third advantage was that, while the valley was protected by high ground everywhere but on the south, it there afforded a large outlook over the boggy basin and the hills beyond its immediate rim, to a horizon in which stood some of the loftier peaks of the highland mountains.

When Steenie's soul was able to banish the nameless forms that haunt the dim borders of insanity, he would sit in that valley for hours, regarding the widespread valley below him, in which he knew every height and hollow. With his exceptionally keen eyesight, he could descry signs of life where another would have beheld but a dead level. It seemed that not a live thing could spread wing or wag tail, but Steenie would become thereby aware of its presence.

Kirsty, boastful to her parents of this faculty of Steenie, said to her father one day, "I dinna believe, father, wi' Steenie on the bog, a red worm could stick up his head oot and him not see 't!"

Steenie set about his house-building at once, and when he had got as far as he could without her, called for help from Kirsty. Divots he was able to cut, and of them he provided a good quality; but when it came to moving stones, two pairs of hands were often wanted. And before the heavier work of "Steenie's hoosie" was over, the two had to beg the help of their father, and of the men from the farm.

During its progress, Phemy Craig paid a rather lengthened visit to Corbyknowe, and often joined the two in their labor on the Horn. She was not very strong, but would carry a good deal in the course of the day, and through this association with Steenie, her dread of him gradually vanished, and they became comrades.

When Steenie's design was at length carried out, they had built up with stone and lime the open spaces between several of the rocks, had cased these curtainwalls outside and lined them inside with softer and warmer walls of divots cut from the green sod of the hill, and had covered in the whole as they found it possible. This done, one of the men who was a good thatcher, fastened the whole roof down with strong lines, so that the wind should not get under and strip it off. The result was a sort of burrow, consisting of several irregular compartments with open communication—or rather, a single chamber composed of recesses. They included one small rock so Steenie could make it serve for a table, and some of its inequalities for shelves. In one of the compartments or recesses, they contrived a fireplace, and in another a tolerably well-concealed exit; for Steenie, like a trap-door spider, could not endure the thought of only one way out. One way was enough for getting in, but another was needful for getting out, his best refuge being the open hill.

The night came at length when Steenie, in whose heart was a solemn, silent jubilation, would take formal possession of his house. It was soft and warm, in the middle of July. The sun had been set for about an hour when he got up to leave the parlor, where the others always sat in the summer, and where Steenie would now and then appear among them. As usual he said good-night to none of them, but stole gently out.

Kirsty knew what was in his mind, but was careful not to show that she took any heed of his departure. As soon as her father and mother retired, she put aside her work and hastened out. She felt a little anxious about him, though she could not have said why. She had no dread of displeasing by joining him. She knew nothing but a sight of the Bonny Man could give him more delight than having her to share his night watch with him. This she had done several times, and they were the only occasions on which, so far as she could tell, he had slept any part of the night.

Folded in the twilight, Earth lay as still and peaceful as if she had never seen anything wrong in one of her children. There was light everywhere, and darkness everywhere to make it strange. A pale green gleam prevailed in the heavens, as if the world were a glowworm that sent abroad its home-born radiance into space, and colored the sky. In the green light rested a few small solid clouds with sharp edges, and almost an assertion of repose. Throughout the night it would be no darker! The sun seemed already to have begun to rise, only he would be all night about it.

The sky was full of pale stars, and Kirsty amused herself, as she went, with arranging them—not into the constellations, though she knew the shapes and names of most of them—but the only stary Steenie knew by name was the polestar, which he always called "the Bonny Man's lantern." Kirsty believed he had thoughts of his own about many others, and names for them too.

She had climbed the hill, and was drawing near the house when she was startled by a sound of something like singing, and stopped to listen. She had never heard Steenie attempt to sing, and the very thought of him doing so moved her greatly—she was always expecting something marvelous to show itself in him. She drew nearer. It was not singing, but something trying to be like it—a succession of broken, harsh, imperfect sounds, with here and there a tone of brief sweetness. The broken music ceased suddenly, and a different kind of sound succeeded. She went yet nearer. He could not be reading; she had tried to teach him to read, but the genuine effort he put forth to learn made his head ache, and his eyes feel wild, he said, and she at once gave up the endeavor. When she reached the door, she could plainly hear him praying.

"Bonny Man, I ken ye weel. There's nobody in heaven or earth that's like Ye! Ye ken Yerself I would die for Ye, if Ye wanted 't o' me, that is, for I'm hopin sore that ye willna want 't. I'm that awful cowardly! O Bonny Man, take the fear oot o' my heart, and make me ready jist to walk off o' the face o' the warld, weighty feet and all, to do Yer will! And eh, Bonny Man, willna Ye come doon sometime, and walk the hill here, that I may look upo' Ye once more—as i' the days of old, when the starlight mountain shook wi' the might o' the prayer Ye heaved up til Yer Father in heaven? Eh, if Ye were but once to look in at the door o' this my hoose that Ye have given me, it would thenceforth be to me as the gate o' paradise! But if Ye *were* to look in at the door, and cry *"Steenie!"* soon would Ye see whether I was in the hoose or no! I thank Ye for this hoose—I'm goin to have a rich and a happy time upo' this hill o' Zion!

"And eh, Bonny Man, give a look i' the face o' my father and mither i' their bed over at the Knowe, and I pray Ye see that Kirsty's gettin a fine sleep, for she has a heap o' tribble wi' me. I'm no worth mindin, yet Ye mind me. She is worth mindin, and that clever, as Ye ken who made her!

"And look upo' this bit hoosie, that I call my own, and they all helped me to build, but as a lean-to til the hoose at home, for I'm no verra far from it or them—jist as that hoose and this hoose and all the hooses are jist but bairnies' hooses, builded by themselves aboot the big flue o' Thy kitchie—wi' Yer ain stanes and divots, Sir."

Steenie's voice ceased, and Kirsty, thinking his prayer had come to an end, knocked at the door, lest her sudden appearance should startle him. From his knees, as she knew by the sound of his rising, Steenie sprang up, and came darting to the door with the cry, "It's Yerself! It's Yerself, Bonny Man!" and seemed to tear it open. Oh, how sorry was Kirsty to stand where the loved of the human was not! She had almost turned and fled.

"It's only me, Steenie!" she faltered, nearly crying.

Steenie stood and stared trembling. For a moment or two neither could speak.

"Eh, Steenie," said Kirsty at length, "I'm right sorry I disappointed ye! I didna ken what I was doin. I ought to have gone hame again!"

"Ye couldna help it," answered Steenie. "Ye couldna be Him, or ye would! But ye're the next best, and right welcome. I'm as glad as can be to see ye, Kirsty. Come away into the hoose."

Kirsty followed him in silence, and sat down dejected. The loving heart saw it.

"Maybe ye're Him after all!" said Steenie. "He can take any shape He likes. I wouldna wonder if ye was Him! Ye're like Him, anyway!"

"Na, na, Steenie! I'm far from that! But I would fain be what He would have me, jist as ye would yerself. So ye must take me, what I am, for His sake, Steenie!"

Although this was the man's hour, and not the dog's, Steenie threw himself at her feet.

"Go oot a bit by yerself, Steenie," she said, caressing him with her hand. "That's what ye like best, I ken! Ye needna mind me! I only came to see ye settled intil yer own hoose. I'll bide a wee bit. Go ye oot, and ken that I'm i' the hoose, and that ye can come back to me when ye like. I have my book, and can sit and read fine."

"Ye're right, Kirsty!" answered Steenie, rising. "I must go oot, for I'm some chokin like. But jist come here a minute first," he went on, leading the way to the door. There he pointed up into the world of stars, and said, "Ye see yon star o' the top o' that other one that's brighter nor itself? Weel, when it comes right over the white top o' yon stane i' the midst o' that side o' the hoose, I shall be here at the door."

Kirsty looked at the stone, saw that the star would arrive at the point indicated in about an hour, and said, "Weel, I'll be expectin ye, Steenie!" whereupon he departed, going farther up the hill to court the soothing of the silent heaven.

In conditions of consciousness known only to himself, the poor fellow sustained an all but continuous hand-to-hand struggle with insanity, more or less agonized according to the nature and force of its varying assault. If not always victorious, he had yet never been defeated in this struggle. Often tempted to escape misery by death, he had hitherto stood firm. Part of every solitary night was spent in fighting that or some other evil suggestion. Doubtless, what kept him lord of himself was his unyielding faith in the Bonny Man.

The name by which he so constantly thought and spoke of the Saviour of men was not of his own finding. The story was well known of the idiot who, having partaken of the Lord's Supper, thought he saw the Saviour, and was heard, as he retired, murmuring to himself, "Eh, Bonny Man, the Bonny Man!" Steenie took up the tale with the most believing mind. Never doubting the man had seen the Lord, he responded with the passionate desire himself to see the Bonny Man. It awoke in him while yet quite a boy, and never left him but, increasing as he grew, became as well it might a fixed idea, a sober, waiting, unebbing passion, urging him to righteousness and lovingkindness.

Kirsty took from her pocket an old translation of Plato's *Phaedo* and sat absorbed in it until the star, unheeded of her, attained its goal, and there was Steenie by her side! She shut the book and rose.

"I'm a heap better, Kirsty," said Steenie. "I'm jist as weel 's there's any need to be. It helped me a heap to ken that ye was sittin here. I could always run til ye! Noo go away to yer bed, and take a guid sleep. I'm thinkin I'll be hame til my breakfast."

"Weel, mother's goin to town the morn, and I'll be wanted. I may as weel go!" answered Kirsty, and without a good-night, or farewell of any sort, for she knew how he felt in regard to leave-takings. Kirsty left him, and went slowly home. The moon was up and so bright that every now and then she would stop for a moment and read a little from her book, and then walk on thinking about it.

From that night, even in the stormy dark of winter, Kirsty was not nearly so anxious about Steenie away from the house. On the Horn he had his place of refuge, and she knew he never ventured on the bog after sunset. He always sought her when he wanted to sleep in the daytime, but he was gradually growing quieter in his mind, and Kirsty had reason to think he slept a good deal more at night.

But the better he grew the more he had the look of one expecting something, and Kirsty often heard him saying to himself, "It's comin! It's comin!"

CHAPTER FIFTEEN

Phemy Craig

Things went on in the same way for four years more, the only visible change being that Kirsty seldomer went about barefooted. She was now between twenty-two and three. Her face, whose ordinary expression had always been quiet, was now quieter still; but when heart or soul was moved, it would flash and glow as only such a face could. Cloud, or shadow of cloud, was hardly to be seen upon it. Her mother, much younger than her father, was still well and strong; and Kirsty, still not much wanted at home, continued to spend the greater part of her time with her brother and her books. As to her person, she was now in the first flower of harmonious womanly strength. Nature had indeed done what she could to make her a lady; but Nature was not her mother, and Kirsty's essential ladyhood came from high up, from the Source itself of Nature. Simple truth was its crown and grace was its garment. To see her walk or run was to look on the divine idea of motion.

As for Steenie, he looked the same loose lank lad as before, with a smile almost too sad to be a smile, and a laugh in which there was little hilarity. His pleasures were no doubt deep and high, but seldom, even to Kirsty, manifested themselves except in the afterglow.

Phemy was almost a woman. She was rather little, but had a

nice figure, which she knew instinctively how to show to the advantage. Her main charm lay in her sweet complexion— strong in its contrast of colors that were wonderfully perfect in their blending. She was gentle of temper, with a shallow, bird-like friendliness, an accentuated confidence that everyone meant her well, which was very taking. But she was far too much pleased with herself to be a necessity to anyone else. Her father grew more and more proud of her, but remained entirely independent of her; and Kirsty could not help wondering at times how he would feel were he given one peep into the chaotic mind which he fancied so lovely a cosmos. A good fairy godmother would for her discipline, Kirsty imagined, turn her into the prettiest wax doll, but with real eyes, and put her in a glass case for the admiration of all, until she sickened of her very consciousness. But Kirsty loved the pretty doll, and cherished any influence she had with her against a possible time when it might be sorely needed. She still encouraged her, therefore, to come to Corbyknowe as often as she felt inclined. Master Craig never interfered with any of her goings and comings. But Kirsty began to notice that Phemy did not care so much for being with her as hitherto.

Phemy had taken more pleasure in her person and appearance, and she regarded other people as much below her. To herself she was the only young lady in Tiltowie, an assurance strengthened by the fact that no young man had yet ventured to court her, which she took as a general admission of their social inferiority, behaving to all the young men the more sweetly in consequence.

The tendency of a weak artistic nature to occupy itself with its own dress was largely developed in her. It was wonderful, considering the smallness of her father's income, how well she arrayed herself. She could make a poor and scanty material go a great way in setting off her attractions. The girls of the neighborhood, not content with complaining that she spent so much time in making her dresses, accused her of spending much money upon them, whereas she spent less than most of them, who cared only for good fabric and the fashion; the fitness to figure and complexion they did not trouble themselves about. The possession of a fine gown was the important thing. As to how it made them look, they had not imagination enough to consider.

Phemy possessed another faculty on which she prided herself far more—the faculty of verse-making. She inherited a certain modicum of her father's rhythmic and rhyming gift. She could string words almost as well as she could string beads, and many thought her clever because she could do what they could not. Her aunt judged her verses marvelous, and her father considered them full of promise. The minister, on the other hand, held them unmistakably silly—as her father would also, had they not been hers and she his. Only the poorest part of his poetic equipment had propagated in her, and had he taught her anything, she would not have overvalued it so much. Herself full of mawkish sentimentality, her verses could not fail to be foolish, their whole impulse being the ambition that springs from self-admiration. She had begun to look down on Kirsty, for she considered her not to be a lady! Neither in speech, manners, nor dress, were she and her mother *genteel!* Their free, hearty, simple bearing, in which was neither smallest roughness nor least suggestion of affected refinement, was not to Phemy's taste, and she began to assume condescending ways.

It was of course a humiliation to Phemy to have an aunt in Mrs. Bremner's humble position, but she loved her after her own feeble fashion; and, although she would willingly have avoided her upon occasion, she went not infrequently to the castle to see her, for the kindhearted woman spoiled her. Not only did she admire Phemy's beauty, and stand amazed at her wonderful cleverness, but she gave from her little store a good part of the money that went to adorn the pretty butterfly. At the same time she offered her the best of advice and imagined Phemy listened to it; but the young who take advice are almost beyond the need of it. Fools must experience a thing themselves before they will believe it; and then, remaining fools, they wonder that their children will not heed their testimony. Faith is the only charm by which the experience of one becomes a vantage ground for the start of another.

CHAPTER SIXTEEN

Sham Love

Through their respect for the memory of his father, the East India Company had just granted Francis Gordon a commission in his father's regiment. In about six weeks he was to try the slight examination required, and then to sail to join it. He had come to see his mother and bid her good-bye. He was no longer a youth, but a handsome young fellow, with a pale face and a rather weary and interesting look. For many months he had been leading an idle life.

One day Phemy went to Castle Weelset to see her aunt and, walking through the garden to find her, met the young laird.

He lifted his hat to Phemy, looked again, and recognized her. They had been friends when she was a child, but since he saw her last she had grown a young woman. She was gliding past him with a pretty bow, and a prettier blush and smile, when he stopped and held out his hand.

"It's not possible!" he said. "You can't be little Phemy! Yet you must be. Why, you're a grown lady! To think how you used to sit on my knee! How is your father?"

Phemy murmured a shy answer and blushed a very flamingo. In her heart she saw before her the very man for her hero. A woman's hero gives some measure not of what she is, but of what she would like to pass for. Here was the ideal for which Phemy had so long been waiting. His glory was his youth, position, and good looks! She gazed up at him with a mixture of shyness and boldness, and Francis saw that she was unusually pretty. He saw also that she was very prettily dressed; and, being one of those men who, imagining themselves gentlemen, feel at liberty to take liberties with a woman socially their inferior, he plucked a narcissus in the border, and said, "Let me finish your dress by adding this to it! Have you got a pin? There! All you wanted to make yourself just perfect!"

Her face was now flaming. She saw he was right in the flower he had chosen, and he saw not only his artistic success but her recognition of it as well, and was gratified. He had a keen feeling of harmony in form and color, and he flattered women by bringing his insight to bear on their dress.

In its new position the flower seemed radiant with something of the same beauty in which it was set. It was like the face above it, and hinted a sympathetic relation with the whole dainty person of the girl. But in truth there was more expression in the flower than was yet in the face. The flower expressed what God was thinking of when He made it; the face what the girl was thinking of herself. When she ceased thinking of herself, then, like the flower, she would show what God was thinking of when He made her.

Francis thought what a dainty little lady she would make if he had the making of her, and at once began talking as he never would had she been what is conventionally called a lady. His familiarity, to which their old acquaintance gave him no right, showed him not his sister's keeper. She was pleased with his presumption, took it for a sign that he regarded her as a lady, and from that moment her head was full of the young laird. She had forgotten all she came about. Lost in delight at his kindness, and yet more at his admiration, she felt as safe in his hands as if he had been her guardian angel. Had he not convinced her that her own notion of herself was correct? Who should know better whether she was a lady, whether she was lovely or not, than this great, handsome, perfect gentleman! Unchecked by any question of propriety, she accompanied him without hesitation into a little arbor at the bottom of the garden, and sat down with him on the bench there provided for the weary and the idle. There they sat, a going-to-be gallant officer bored to death by being at home with his mother, and a girl who spent the most of her time in making, altering, and wearing her dresses.

"How good it was of you, Phemy," he said, "to come and see me! I was ready to cut my throat for want of something pretty to look at. I was thinking it the ugliest place with the ugliest people, wondering how I had ever been able to live in it. How unfair I was! The whole country is beautiful now!"

"I am so glad," answered poor Phemy, hardly knowing what she said. It was to her the story of a sad gentleman who fell in love at first sight with a beautiful lady who was learning to love him through pity.

Her admiration of him was as clear as the red and white on her face, and foolish Francis felt in his turn flattered, for he too was fond of himself. There is no more pitiable sight to lovers of their kind, than two persons falling into love rooted in self-love. But possibly they are neither to be pitied nor laughed at; they may be plunging thus into a saving hell.

"You would like to make the world beautiful for me, Phemy?" rejoined Francis.

"I should like to make it a paradise!" returned Phemy.

"A garden of Eden, and you the Eve in it?" suggested Francis.

Phemy could find no answer beyond a confused look and a yet deeper blush.

Talk elliptical followed, not unmingled with looks bold and shy. They had not many objects of thought in common, therefore not many subjects for conversation. There was no poetry in Francis, and but the flimsiest sentiment in Phemy. Her mind was feebly active, his full of tedium. Hers was open to any temptation from him, and his to the temptation of usurping the government of her world, of constituting himself the benefactor of this innocent creature, and enriching her life with the bliss of loving a noble object. Of course he meant nothing serious! Equally of course he would do her no harm! To lose him would make her miserable for a while, but she would not die of love, and would have something to think about all her dull life afterward!

At length Phemy got frightened at the thought of being found with him, and together they went to look for her aunt. Finding her in a back building that was used for laundry, Francis told Mrs. Bremner that they had been in the garden ever so long searching for her, and he was very glad of the opportunity of hearing about his old friend, Phemy's father! The aunt was not quite pleased, but said little.

The following Sunday, she told the schoolmaster what had taken place, and came home in a rage at the idiocy of a man who would not open his eyes when his house was on fire. It was all her sister's fault, she said, for having married such a book-idiot! She felt very uncomfortable, and did her best in the way of warning, but Phemy seemed so incapable of understanding what ill could come of letting the young laird talk to her, that she despaired of rousing in her any sense of danger; and having no authority over her, she was driven to silence for the present. She would have spoken to Francis' mother, but knew it would be of no use; she would either laugh, and say young men must have their way, or fly into a fury with Phemy for trying to entrap *her* son. One thing was certain—if his mother opposed him, Francis would persist.

CHAPTER SEVENTEEN

A Novel Abduction

Phemy seldom went to the castle, but she and the young laird met often. There was solitude enough in that country for an army of lovers. Once or twice, at Phemy's entreaty, Francis went and took tea with her at her father's, and was cordially received by the schoolmaster, who had no sense of impropriety in their strolling out together afterward, leaving him well content with the company of his books. Before this had happened twice, all the town was talking about it, and predicting evil. Phemy heard nothing and feared nothing. So rapidly did the whirlwind of tongues extend its gyration that within half a week it reached Kirsty, and cast her into great trouble. Her poor silly defenseless Phemy, the child of her friend, was in danger from the son of her father's friend! Her father could do nothing, for Francis would not listen to him, therefore she herself must do something! She could not sit still and look on at the devil's work!

Having always been on terms of sacred intimacy with her mother, she knew more of the dangers of the world than most girls, and understood perfectly that an unwise man is not to be trusted with a foolish girl. She felt that inaction on her part would be faithlessness to the teaching of her mother, as well as treachery to her father, whose friend's son was in peril of doing a fearful wrong to one whom he owed almost a brother's protection for his schoolmaster's sake. She did not believe that Francis *meant* Phemy any harm, but she was certain he thought too much of himself to marry her; and were the poor child's feelings to go for nothing? She had no hope that Phemy would listen to expostulation from her, but she must in fairness, before she *did* anything, have some speech with her!

She made repeated efforts to see her, but without success. She tried one time of day after another, but, now by accident and now by clever contrivance, Phemy was not at home. She had of late grown tricky. One of the windows of the schoolmaster's house commanded the street in both directions, and Phemy commanded the window. When she saw Kirsty coming, she would run into the garden and take refuge in the summerhouse, telling the servant on her way that she was going out, and did not know what time she would be in. On more occasions than one Kirsty said she would wait. When Phemy learned she was not gone, she went out in earnest, and took care Kirsty had enough of waiting. Such shifts of cunning showed that Phemy was in some degree afraid of Kirsty.

Kirsty was certain that it would be almost impossible to rouse the schoolmaster. He would be utterly furious that his confidence had been abused, and probably bear himself in such fashion as to make Phemy desperate, perhaps making her hate him. As it was, he turned a deaf ear and indignant heart to every one of the reports that reached him. To listen to it would be to doubt his child! Why should not the young laird fall in love with her? What was more natural? He cursed the gossips of the town and returned to his book.

Convinced at length that Phemy declined an interview, Kirsty resolved to take her own way. And her way was a somewhat masterful one.

About a mile from Castle Weelset, in the direction of Tiltowie, the road was close-flanked by steep heathery braes for a few hundred yards. Kirsty had heard of Phemy's being several times on this road of late; and near this particular spot, she resolved to waylay her. From the brae on the side next to Corbyknowe she could see the road for some distance in either direction.

For a week she watched in vain. She saw the two pass together more than once, and she saw Francis pass alone, but she had never seen Phemy alone.

One morning, just as she arrived at her usual outlook, she saw Mrs. Bremner in the road below, coming from the castle, and ran down to speak to her. In the course of their conversation she learned that Francis was to start for London the next morning. When they parted, the woman resuming her walk to Tiltowie, Kirsty climbed the brae and sat down in the heather. She was more anxious than ever. She had done her best, but it had come to nothing, and now she had but one chance more! The impending departure of Francis Gordon was good news, but much could still happen yet even before he went! At the same time she could think of nothing better than to keep watch as hitherto for Phemy, but now determined to speak to both if Francis was with her, and all but determined to speak to Francis alone, if an opportunity of doing so should be given her.

All morning and afternoon she watched in vain, eating nothing but a piece of bread that Steenie brought her. At last, in the cool September evening, the sun down, and a melancholy glory hanging over the place of his vanishing, she spied the solitary form of Phemy hastening along the road in the direction of the castle. She waited until she was at the precise spot, and leaped into the road a few feet in front of her—so suddenly that the girl started with a cry, and stopped. The moment she saw who it was, however, she drew herself up, and would have passed with a stiff greeting. But Kirsty stood in front of her and would not permit her.

"What do you want, Kirsty Barclay?" demanded Phemy, who had within the last week or two advanced considerably in confidence of manner. "I am in a hurry!"

"Ye're in a worse hurry than ye ken, for yer hurry should be the other way!" answered Kirsty. "I'm goin to turn ye, or at least no goin to let ye go, til ye hear a bit o' the truth from a woman older nor yerself! Lassie, ye seem to think nobody worth hearkenin til 'cept a man, but I mean ye to hearken to me! Ye dinna ken what ye're aboot! I ken Francie Gordon a heap better nor you, and though I ken no ill o' him, I ken as little guid. He never did nothin yet but to please himself, and there never came salvation or comfort to man, woman, or bairn by any poor creature like *him!*"

"How dare you speak such lies of a gentleman behind his back!" cried Phemy, her eyes flashing. "He is a friend of mine, and I will not hear him maligned!"

"There's a small harm can come to any man from the truth, Phemy!" answered Kirsty. "Set the man afore me, and I'll say word intil his face what I'm saying to you ahind his back."

"Miss Barclay," rejoined Phemy, with a rather pitiable attempt at dignity, "I can permit no one to call me by my Christian name who speaks ill of the man to whom I am engaged!"

"That shall be as ye please, Miss Craig. But I would let you call me all the ill names in the dictionary to get ye to hearken to me! I'm tellin ye nothin but what's true as death."

"I call no one names. I am always civil to my neighbors whoever they may be! I will not listen to you."

"Eh, lassie, there's but few o' yer neighbors civil to yer name, whatever they be to yerself! There's hardly one has a guid word for ye, Phemy—Miss Craig—I beg yer pardon!"

"Their lying tongues are nothing to me! I know what I am about! I will not stay a moment longer with you! I have an important engagement." And once more, as several times already, she would have passed, but Kirsty stepped yet again in front of her.

"I can weel take yer word," replied Kirsty, "that ye have an engagement, but ye said a minute ago that ye was engaged til him. Tell me in a word—has Francie Gordon promised to marry ye?"

"He has as good as asked me," answered Phemy, who had fits of apprehensive recoil from a downright lie.

"Noo there I could a'most believe ye! Ay, that would be ill enough for Francie! He was never a doonright liar, so long's I kenned him—anymore nor yerself! But dinna imagine he'll every marry ye, for that he will not."

"This is really insufferable!" cried Phemy, in a voice that

began to tremble from the approach of angry tears. "Pray, have *you* a claim upon him?"

"None, no a shadow o' one," returned Kirsty. But my father and his were like brithers, and we have all to do what we can for his father's son. I would fain hold him for gettin into trouble wi' you or any lass."

"*I* get him into trouble! Really, Miss Barclay, I do not know how to understand you!"

"I see I must be plain wi' ye. I wouldna have ye get him into trouble by lettin him get you into trouble, and that's plain speakin!"

"You insult me!" said Phemy.

"Ye drive me to speak plain!" answered Kirsty. "That lad, Francie Gordon—"

"Speak with respect of your superiors," interrupted Phemy.

"I'll speak wi' respect o' anybody I have respect for!" answered Kirsty.

"Let me pass, you rude young woman!" cried Phemy, who had of late been cultivating in her imagination such speech as she thought would befit Mrs. Gordon of Castle Weelset.

"I willna let ye pass," answered Kirsty, "that is, no til ye hear what I have to say to ye."

"Then you must take the conseqences!" rejoined Phemy, and, in the hope that her lover would prove within earshot, began a piercing scream.

This roused something in Kirsty which she could not afterward identify. She was sure it had nothing to do with anger, and did nothing but what she had beforehand resolved upon. She felt as if she had to deal with a child who insisted on playing with fire beside a barrel of gunpowder. She caught up the little would-be lady, as if she had been that same naughty child, and with the suddenness of the action so astonished Phemy that for a moment or two she neither moved nor uttered a sound. However, she then began to shriek and struggle wildly, as if in the hug of a bear, whereupon Kirsty covered her mouth with one hand while she held her fast with the other. It was a violent proceeding, but Kirsty chose to be thus far an offender.

Bearing her as best she could in one arm, she ran with her to a place where the road was bordered by a more gentle slope. There she took to the moorland, and made for Corbyknowe. Her resolve had been from the first, if Phemy would not listen, to carry her, like the unmanageable child she was, home to the mother whose voice had always been to herself the oracle of God. Her heart beat mightily with love and labor, as she waded through the heather, hurrying along the moor.

It was a strange abduction, but Kirsty was divinely simple. Not until they were out of sight of the road did she set her down.

"Noo, Phemy," she said, panting as she spoke, "Hold yer tongue like a guid lassie, and come away upo' yer own feet."

Phemy took at once to her heels and her throat, and ran shrieking back toward the road, with Kirsty after her like a grayhound. Phemy had for some time given up struggling and trying to shriek, and was therefore in better breath than Kirsty whose lungs were pumping hard. But Phemy had not a chance, for there was more muscle in one of Kirsty's legs than in her whole body. In a moment Kirsty had her in her arms again, and so fast that she could not even kick. She gave way and burst into tears, and Kirsty relaxed her hold.

"What are you goin to do wi' me?" sobbed Phemy.

"I'm takin ye to the best place I ken—hame to my mither," answered Kirsty, striding on for home as straight as she could go.

"I willna go!" cried Phemy, whose Scotch had returned with her tears.

"Ye *are* goin," returned Kirsty dryly. "At least I'm takin ye, and that's next best."

"What for? I never did ye an ill turn that I ken o'!" said Phemy, and burst afresh into tears of self-pity and sense of wrong.

"Na, my bonny lassie," answered Kirsty, "ye never did me any ill turn! But that's not the less reason that I shouldna do you a guid one! And yer father has been like the Bountiful Himself to me! It's no muckle I can do for you or for him, but there's a thing I'm set upo', and that's holdin ye from Francie Gordon the night. He'll be away the morn!"

"Who telled ye that?" returned Phemy with a start.

"Jist yer own aunt, honest woman!" answered Kirsty.

"She might have held the tongue o' her till he was gone! It's nothin but ye're envious o' me, Kirsty, 'cause ye canna get him yerself! He would never look at a lass like you!"

Kirsty's answer was silence. Phemy then tried entreaty.

"Let me go, Kirsty! Please! I'll go doon o' my knees til ye! I canna bide him to think I've played him false."

"He'll play you false, my lamb, whatever ye do or ye think! It makes my heart sore to ken that no guid will your heart get o' his. He shall no see ye the night, anyway!"

Phemy uttered a childish howl, but immediately choked it with a proud sob.

"Ye're hurtin me, Kirsty!" she said, after a minute or so of silence. "Let me doon, and I'll go straight hame to my father. I promise ye."

"I'll set ye doon," answered Kirsty, "but ye must come hame to my mither."

"What'll my father think?"

"I shall no forget yer father," said Kirsty.

She sent out a strange, piercing cry, set Phemy down, took her hand in hers, and went on, Phemy making no resistance. In about three minutes there was a noise in the heather, and Snootie came rushing to Kirsty. A few moments more and Steenie appeared. He lifted his bonnet to Phemy, and stood waiting his sister's commands.

"Steenie," she said, "take the dog wi' ye, and run doon to the toon, and tell Mr. Craig that Phemy here's comin hame wi' me, to bide the night. Ye willna be longer nor ye canna help, and ye'll come to the hoose afore ye go to the hill?"

"I'll do that, Kirsty. Come, doggie."

Steenie never went to the town of his own accord, and Kirsty never liked him to go, for the boys were rude, but tonight it would be dark before he reached it.

"Ye're no surely goin to make me bide all night!" said Phemy, beginning again to cry.

"I am that—the night, and maybe the morn's night, and any number o' nights till we're sure he's away!" answered Kirsty, resuming her walk.

Phemy wept aloud, but did not try to escape.

"And him goin to promise this very night that he would marry me!" she cried, but through her tears and sobs her words were indistinct.

Kirsty stopped, and faced round on her. "He promised to marry ye?" she said.

"I didna say that. I said he was goin to promise the night. And noo he'll be gone, and never a word said!"

"He promised, did he, that he would promise the night? Eh, Francie, Francie! Ye're no yer father's son! He promised to promise to marry ye! Eh, ye poor gowk o' a bonny lassie!" All Kirsty's inborn motherhood awoke. She turned to her, clasped the silly thing in her arms, cried out, "Puir wee dauty! If he have a heart any bigger nor the fox's own, he'll come to ye to the Knowe, and say what he has to say!"

"He willna ken where I am!" answered Phemy with an agonized burst of dry sobbing.

"Will he noo? I shall see to that—and this very night!" exclaimed Kirsty. "I'll give him every chance o' doin the right thing!"

"But he'll be angered at me!"

"What for? Did he tell ye no to tell?"

"Ay he did."

"Worse and worse!" cried Kirsty indignantly. "He would have ye all in his grip! He telled ye, no doobt, that ye was the bonniest lassie that ever was seen! Jist tell me, Phemy, dinna ye think a heap more o' yerself since he took ye in hand?"

She would have Phemy see that she had gathered from him no figs or grapes, only thorns and thistles.

Phemy made no reply. Had she not every right to think well of herself? He had never said anything to her on that subject which she was not quite ready to believe.

Kirsty seemed to divine what was passing in her thought.

"A man," she said, "that doesna tell ye the truth aboot

himself's no likely to tell ye the truth aboot *yerself!* Did he tell ye hoo many lassies he had said the same thing til afore ever he came to you? It mattered little so long as they were lassies as heartless as himself, and over weel used to sic talk. But a lassie like you, that never afore heared siclike, she takes them all for truth! Ye're jist a bonnie lassie, siclike as many anither. But if ye were all glorious within, like the Queen o' Sheba, or whatever she may happen to have been, there would be nothing to be proud o' i' that, seeing ye didna contrive yerself."

Phemy was incapable of understanding such a statement and deduction. If she was lovely, as Francis told her, and as she saw in the glass, why should she not be pleased with herself? If Kirsty had been made like her, she would have been just as vain as she!

All her life the doll never saw the beauty of the woman. Beside Phemy, Kirsty walked like an Olympian goddess beside the naiad of a brook. And Kirsty was a goddess, for she was what she had to be, and never thought about it.

Phemy sank down in the heather, declaring she could go no farther, and looked so white and so pitiful that Kirsty's heart filled afresh with compassion. Like the mother she was, she took the poor girl yet again in her arms, and, carrying her quite easily now that she did not struggle, walked with her straight into her mother's kitchen.

Mrs. Barclay sat darning the stocking which would have been Kirsty's affair had she not been stalking Phemy. She took it out of her mother's hands, and laid the girl in her lap.

"There's a new bairnie, mither! Ye must dote on her a wee, for she's verra tired!" she said, and seating herself on a stool, went on with the darning of the stocking.

Mistress Barclay looked down on Phemy with such a face of loving benignity that the poor miserable girl threw her arms round her neck and laid her head on her bosom.

Instinctively the mother began to hush and soothe her, and in a moment more was singing a lullabye to her. Phemy fell fast asleep. Then Kirsty told what she had done, and while she spoke, the mother sat silent, brooding and hushing and thinking.

CHAPTER EIGHTEEN

Phemy's Champion

When she had told all, Kirsty rose, and laying aside the stocking said, "I'm away to Weelset, mither. I promised the bairn I would let Francie ken where she was, and give him the chance o' sayin his say til her."

"Very weel, lassie! Ye ken what ye're aboot, and I shall no interfere wi' ye. But, eh, ye'll be tired afore ye go to yer bed!"

"I'll no tramp it, mither. I'll take the gray mare."

"She's fresh, lassie; ye must be on yer guard."

"All the better!" returned Kirsty. "To hear ye, mither, a body would think I couldna ride!"

"Forbid it, bairn! Yer father says, man or woman, there's no one i' the countryside like ye upo' beastback."

"They take to me, the creatures! It was themselves learned me to ride!" answered Kirsty, as she took a riding whip from the wall, and went out of the kitchen.

The mare looked round when Kirsty entered the stable, and whinnied. Kirsty petted and stroked her, gave her two or three handfuls of oats, and while she was eating strapped a cloth on her back. There was no sidesaddle about the farm, and although Kirsty could ride well enough sideways, she liked the way her father had taught her far better. Utterly fearless, she had grown a horsewoman such as few.

The moment the mare had finished her oats, Kirsty bridled her, led her out, sprang on her back, and rode quietly out of the farmyard. The moment she was beyond the gate, she leaned back and, throwing her right foot over the mare's crest, rode like an Amazon, at ease and with mastery. The same moment the mare was away, up hill and down dale, almost at racing speed. Had the coming moon been above the horizon, the Amazon farm girl would have been worth meeting! So perfectly did she yield her lithe, strong body to every motion of the mare, abrupt or undulant, that neither ever felt a jar, and their movements seemed the outcome of a vital force common to the two. Kirsty never thought about her riding, but the mare knew that all was right between them. Kirsty never touched bridle except to moderate the mare's pace when she was too excited to heed what she said to her.

Doubtless, to many eyes, she would have looked better in a riding habit, but she would have felt like an eagle in a nightgown. She wore a full winsey petticoat, and stockings of the same color.

On her head she had nothing but the silk net worn by young unmarried women. In the rush of the gallop it slipped, and its contents escaped. She put the net in her pocket, and cast a knot upon her long hair as if it had been a rope. This she did without even slackening her speed, transferring the whip she carried from her hand to her teeth. It was one Colonel Gordon had given her father in remembrance of a little adventure they had together, in which a lash from it in the dark night was mistaken for a sword cut, and did them no small service.

By the time they reached the castle, the moon was above the horizon. Kirsty brought the mare to a walk, and resuming her pillion seat, remanded her hair to its cage and readjusted her skirt. Then settling herself as in a sidesaddle, she rode gently up to the castle door.

A manservant, happening to see her from the hall window, saved her having to ring the bell and greeted her respectfully, for everybody knew Corbyknowe's Kirsty. She said she wanted to see Mr. Gordon, and suggested that perhaps he would be kind enough to speak to her at the door. The man went to find his master, and in a minute or two brought the message that Mr. Gordon would be with her presently. Kirsty drew her mare back into the shadow, and waited.

It was three minutes before Francis came sauntering bare-headed round the corner of the house, his hands in his pockets, and a cigar in his mouth. He gave a glance round, not seeing his visitor at once, and then with a nod, came toward her, still smoking. His nonchalance was forced and meant to cover uneasiness. For all that had passed to make him forget Kirsty, he yet remembered her uncomfortably, and at the present moment could not help regarding her as an angelic *bête noir,* of whom he was more afraid than of any other human being. He approached her in a sort of sidling stroll, as if he had no actual business with her, but thought of just asking whether she would sell her horse. He did not speak, and Kirsty sat motionless until he was near enough for a low-voiced conference.

"What are ye aboot wi' Phemy Craig, Francie?" she began, without a word of greeting.

Kirsty was one of the few who practically deny time. She spoke to the tall handsome young man in the same tone and with the same forms as when they were boy and girl together.

He had meant their conversation to be at arm's length, so to say, but his intention broke down at once, and he answered her in the same style.

"I ken nothin aboot her. What for should I?" he answered.

"I ken ye dinna ken where she is," returned Kirsty. "Ye answer the question! What are ye aboot wi' Phemy, I challenge ye again! Poor lassie, she has no brither to say the word!"

"That's all very weel, but ye see, Kirsty," he began, then stopped, and having stared at her a moment in silence, exclaimed, "What a splendid woman you've grown!" He had probably been drinking with his mother.

Kirsty sat speechless, motionless, changeless as a soldier on guard. Gordon had to resume and finish his sentence.

"As I was going to say, *you* can't take the place of a brother to her, Kirsty, else I should know how to answer you! It's awkward when a lady takes you to task," he added with a drawl.

"Dinna trouble yer head aboot that, Francie," rejoined Kirsty. Then changing to English as he had done, she went on. "I claim no consideration on that score."

Francis Gordon felt very uncomfortable. It was deuced hard to be bullied by a woman! He stood silent, because he had nothing to say.

"Do you mean to marry Phemy?" asked Kirsty.

"Really, Miss Barclay," Francis began, but Kirsty interrupted him.

"Mr. Gordon," she said sternly, "be a man, and answer me. If you mean to marry her, say so, and go and tell her father—or my father, if you prefer. She is at the Knowe, miserable that she did not meet you tonight. That was my doing—she could not help herself."

Gordon broke into a strained laugh. "Well, you've got her and you can keep her!" he said.

"You have not answered my question!"

"Really, Miss Barclay, you must not be too hard upon a man. Is a fellow not to speak to a woman but he must say at once whether or not he intends to marry her?"

"Answer my question."

"It is a ridiculous one."

"You have been trysting with her almost every night for something like a month!" rejoined Kirsty. "The question is not at all ridiculous."

"Let it be granted then, and let the proper person ask me the question, and I will answer it. You, pardon me, have nothing to do with the matter."

"That is the answer of a coward," returned Kirsty, her cheek flaming at last. "You know the guileless nature of your old schoolmaster, and take advantage of it! You know that the poor girl has not a man to look to, and you will not have a woman befriend her! It is cowardly, ungrateful, mean, and treacherous. You are a bad man, Francie! You were always a fool, but now you are a wicked fool! If I were her brother—if I were a man, I would thrash you!"

"It's a good thing you're not able, Kirsty! I should be frightened!" said Gordon, with a laugh and a shrug, thinking to throw the thing aside as done with.

"I said, if I were a man!" returned Kirsty. "I did not say, if I were able! I *am* able." And to herself she added, "I don't see why a woman should leave to any man what she's able to do for herself!"

"Francie, you're no gentleman. You're a scoundrel and a coward!" she immediately added aloud.

"Very well," returned Francis angrily. "Since you choose to be treated as a man and tell me I am no gentleman, I tell you I wouldn't marry the girl if the two of you went on your knees to me! A common, silly, countrybred flirt—ready for anything a man—"

Kirsty's whip descended upon him with a merciless lash. The hiss of it, as it cut the air with all the force of her strong arm, startled her mare and she sprang aside, so that Kirsty, who had thrown the strength of her whole body into the blow, could not but lose her seat. But it was only to stand upright on her feet, fronting her antagonist. Gordon was grasping his head—the blow had for a moment blinded him. She gave him another stinging cut across the hands.

"That's from yer father! The whip was his, and his sword never did fairer work!" she said. "I have done for him what I could!" she added in a low sorrowful voice, and stepped back, as having fulfilled her mission.

He rushed at her with a sudden torrent of evil words. But he was no match for her agility. She avoided him as she had more than once a charging bull, every now and then dealing him another sharp blow from his father's whip. The treatment began to bring him to his senses.

"Kirsty!" he cried, ceasing his attempts to lay hold of her. "Stop, or we'll have the whole hoose oot, and what'll come o' me then I darena think! I doobt I'll never hear the last o' 't as 'tis!"

"Am I to trust ye, Francie?"

"I willna lay a finger upo' ye, damn ye!" he said in mingled wrath and humiliation.

Throughout, Kirsty had held her mare by the bridle, and she, although behaving as well as she could, had, in the fright the laird's rushes and the sounds of the whip caused her, added not a little to her mistress's difficulties. Just as Kirsty sprang on her back, the door opened and faces looked peering out. With a cut or two Kirsty encouraged a few wild gambols, so that all the trouble would appear to have been with the mare. Then she rode quietly through the gate.

Gordon stood in a motionless fury until he heard the soft thunder of the mare's hoofs on the turf as Kirsty rode home at a fierce gallop. Then he turned and went into the house, not to communicate what had taken place, but to lie about it as like truth as he might find possible.

About halfway home, on the side of a hill, across which a low wind blew with a hopeless, undulant death moan of autumn among the heather, Kirsty broke into a passionate fit of weeping. But before she reached home all traces of her tears had vanished.

Gordon did not go the next day, nor the day after, but he never saw Phemy again. It was a week before he showed himself, and then he was not a beautiful sight. He attributed one visible wale on his cheek and temple to a blow from a twig as he ran in the dusk through the shrubbery after a strange dog. Even at the castle they did not know exactly when he left it. His luggage was sent after him

The domestics were perplexed as to the wale on his face, until the man to whom Kirsty had spoken at the door hazarded a conjecture or two. It was not far from the truth, and as such accepted; the general admiration and respect which already haloed Corbyknowe's Kirsty were now mingled with a little wholesome fear.

When Kirsty told her father and mother what she had done at Castle Weelset, neither said a word. Her mother turned her head away; but the light in her father's eyes, had she any doubt as to how they would take it, would have put her quite at ease.

CHAPTER NINETEEEN

Francis Gordon's Champion

Poor little Phemy was in bed, and had cried herself asleep. Kirsty was more tired than she had ever been before. She went to bed at once, but for a long time could not sleep.

She had no doubt her parents approved of the chastisement she had given Francis, and she herself nowise repented of it; yet the instant she lay down, back came the sudden something that set her weeping on the hillside. As then, all unsent for, the face of Francie Gordon, such as he was in their childhood, rose before her, but marred by her hand with stripes of disgrace from his father's whip; and with the vision came again the torrent of her tears; for, if his father had then struck him so, she would have been bold in his defense. She pressed her face into the pillow lest her sobs should be heard. She was by no means a young woman ready to weep, but the thought of the boy-face, with her blows upon it, got within her guard and ran her through the heart. It seemed as if nevermore would she escape the imagined sight. It is a sore thing when a woman, born a protector, has for protection to become an avenger; and severe was the revulsion in Kirsty from an act of violence foreign to the whole habit, though nowise inconsistent with the character, of the calm, thoughtful woman. She had never struck even the one-horned cow that would, for very cursedness, kick over the milkpail! Hers was the wrath of the mother, whose very presence in a calm soul is its justification—for how could it be there but by the original energy? The wrath was gone, and the mother-soul turned against itself—not in judgment at all, but in irrepressible feeling. She did not for one moment think that she ought not to have done it, and she was glad in her heart to know that what he had said and she had done must keep Phemy and him apart; but there was the blow on the face of the boy she loved, and there was the reflex wound in her own soul! Surely she loved him yet with her mother-love, else how could she have been angry enough with him to strike him!

For weeks the pain lasted keen, and it was ever after ready to return. It was a human type of the divine suffering in the discipline of the sinner, which with some of the old prophets takes the shape of God's repenting of the evils He has brought on His people; and it was the only trouble she ever kept from her mother—she feared to wake her own pain in the dearer heart. She could have told her father; for, although he was just as loving as her mother, he was not so softhearted, and would not distress himself too much about an ache more or less in a heart that had done its duty. But as she could not tell her mother, she would not tell her father. Her parents saw that a change had passed upon her, and partially understood the nature of it. They perceived that she left behind her on that night a measure of her gaiety, that thereafter she was yet gentler to her parents, and if possible yet tenderer to her brother.

Although Kirsty had manifested her superiority of character in her relations with Francis, the feeling was never absent from her that he was of a race above her own; and now the visage of the young officer in her father's old regiment never rose in her mind's eye uncrossed by the livid mark of her whip from the temple down the cheek! Whether she had actually seen it so, she did not remember; but so it always came to her. And the face of the man never cost her a tear—it was only that of the boy that made her weep.

Another thing distressed her even more. The instant before she struck him first, she saw on his face an expression so meanly

selfish that she felt as if she hated him. That expression had
vanished from her visual memory, her whip had wiped it away,
but she knew that for a moment she had all but hated him—if it
was indeed *all but!*

All the house was careful the next morning that Phemy
should not be disturbed; and when at length the poor child
appeared, her color so washed out by tears, Kirsty made haste to
get her a nice breakfast, and would answer none of her questions until she had made a proper meal.

"Noo, Kirsty," said Phemy at last, "ye must tell me what he
said when ye let him ken that I couldna go til him 'cause ye
wouldna let me!"

"He saidna muckle to that. I dinna think he had been sore
missin ye."

"I see ye're no goin to tell me the truth, Kirsty! I ken by myself
he must have been missin me dreadful!"

"Ye can judge no man by yerself, Phemy. Men's no like lass-
fowk."

Phemy laughed. "What ken *ye* aboot men, Kirsty?"

"I'm no pretendin to any experience," returned Kirsty. "I
would only have ye take counsel wi' common sense. Is 't likely,
Phemy, that a man wi' grand relations, an grand notions, a man
wi' a fourth o' great ladies in his acquaintance to make a fool o'
him and themselves thegither, special noo that he's an officer i'
the Company's service— is't any way likely, I say, that he should
be as muckle taken wi' a wee bit country lassie as she couldna but
be wi' him?"

"Noo, Kirsty, ye jist needna go aboot to make me mistrust one
who's the very mirror o' all knightly courtesy." rejoined Phemy,
speaking out of the highflown, thin atmosphere she thought the
region of poetry, "for ye canna! Nothin ever anybody said could
make me think different o' *him!*"

"Nor nothin ever he said himself?" asked Kirsty.

"Nothin," answered Phemy, with strength and decision.

"No if't was that nothin would ever make him marry ye?"

"That he might weel say, for he willna need makin! But he
never said it, and ye needna try to throw it upo' me!" she added,

in a tone that showed the very idea too painful.

"He did say 't, Phemy."

"Who telled ye? It's lies! Somebody's lyin!"

"He said it til me himself. Never a lie had anybody had a chance o' puttin intil the tale!"

"He never said 't, Kirsty!" cried Phemy, her cheeks now glowing, now pale as death. "He darena!"

"He dared, and he dared to *me!* He said, 'I wouldna marry her if both o' ye went doon upo' yer knees to me!' "

"Ye must have sore angered him, Kirsty, or he wouldna have said it! Of course he wasna to be guided by you! He couldna have meaned what he said! He would never have said it til me! I wish wi' all my heart I hadna let ye go til him! Ye have ruined all!"

"Ye never let me go, Phemy! It was my business to go."

"I see what's intil 't!" cried Phemy, bursting into tears. "Ye telled him hoo little ye thought o' me, and that made him change his mind!"

"Would he be worth grievin aboot if that were the case, Phemy? But ye ken it wasna that! Ye ken that I jist couldna do anythin o' the sort."

"Hoo am I to ken? There's no a woman born but would fain have him til hersel!"

Kirsty held her peace for pity, thinking what she could say to convince her of Gordon's faithlessness.

"He didna say he hadna promised?" resumed Phemy through her sobs.

"We camna upo' that."

"What did ye give him, Kirsty, when he told ye—no that I believe a word o' 't—that he would have none o' me?"

Kirsty laughed with a scorn none the less clear that it was quiet. "Jist a guid lickin," she answered.

"Ha, ha!" laughed Phemy hysterically. "I telled ye ye was lyin! Ye have been nothin but lyin—all for fun, of course I ken that— to make a fool o' me for bein fleyt!"

For a moment despair seemed to overwhelm Kirsty. Was it for this she had so wounded her own soul? How was she to make the poor child understand? She lifted up her heart in silence. At last she said, "Ye willna see more o' him this year or twa anyway, I'm thinkin! If ever ye hear from 'is pen, it'll surprise me. But if ever ye have the chance, which may God forbid, tell him I said I had given him his licks, and dare him to come and deny 't to my face. He willna do that, Phemy! He kens over weel I would jist give him them again!"

"He would kill ye, Kirsty! *You* give him his licks!"

"He might kill me, but he'd have a part o' his licks first! And noo if ye dinna believe me, I willna answer a single question more ye put to me. I have been tellin ye the truth, it's sure, and it's no use, for ye willna believe a word o' 't!"

Phemy rose in a fury.

"And ye laid hand to cheek o' that king o' men, Kirsty Barclay? Lord, hold me or I'll kill her! Little holds me from tearin ye to bits wi' my twa hands!"

"I laidna hand to cheek o' Francie Gordon, Phemy! I jist thrashed him wi' his father's own ridin whip that my heart's like to break to think o' 't. I doobt he'll carry the marks til his grave." And Kirsty broke into a convulsion of silent sobs and tears.

"Kirsty Barclay, ye're a deevil!" cried Phemy in a hoarse whisper. She was spent with passion.

The little creature stood before Kirsty, her hands clenched and shaking with rage, blue flashes darting about her eyes. Kirsty, at once controlling the passion of her own heart, sat still as a statue, regarding her with a sad pity.

Phemy cried, "I'll be cursin all the warld and God Himself, if I go on this way! Eh, ye false woman!"

Kirsty sprang upon her at one bound from her seat, threw her arms round her so that she could not move hers, and sitting down with her on her lap, said, "Phemy, if I was yer mither, I would give ye yer licks for sayin what ye didna i' yer heart believe! All the time ye was keepin company wi' Francie Gordon, ye ken i' yer own soul ye was never right sure o' him! And noo I tell ye plainly that I struck him times and times wi' my whip. Do not believe him so ill-contrived as ye would make me think him. Him and me was bairns thegither, and I ken the nature o' him, and take his part again ye, for, out o' pride and ambition, ye're an enemy til him. I do not believe ever he promised to marry ye! He's behavin ill enough wantin that—lettin a gowk o' a lassie like you believe what ye liked, and him only carryin on wi' ye for the play o' 't, havin nothin to do. A man's word's his word, and Francie's no so ill as your tale would make him! There, Phemy, I have said my say!"

She loosened her arms. But Phemy lay still, and putting her arms round Kirsty's neck, wept in bitter silence.

CHAPTER TWENTY

Mutual Ministration

In a minute or so the door opened, and Steenie coming one step into the kitchen, stood and stared with such a face of concern that Kirsty was obliged to speak. He had never seen a woman weeping. He shivered visibly.

"Phemy's no that weel," she said, "Her heart's so sore it makes her grieve. She canna help grievin, poor darlin!"

Phemy lifted her face from Kirsty's bosom, where, like a miserable child, she had been pressing it hard; and, seeming to have lost in the depth of her grief all her natural shyness, she looked at Steenie with the most pitiful look ever countenance wore, and her rage turned to self-commiseration. The cloud of mingled emotion and distress on the visage of Steenie wavered, shifted, changed, and settled into the divinest look of pity and protection. He turned away from them and, his head bent upon his breast, stood for a time utterly motionless. Even Phemy, overpowered and stilled by that last look he cast upon her, gazed at him with involuntary reverence. But only Kirsty knew that the half-witted had sought and found audience with the Eternal, and was now in His presence.

He remained in this position about three minutes. Then he lifted his head, and without a word walked straight from the house. Kirsty did not go after him, for she feared to tread on holy ground uninvited; neither would she leave Phemy until her mother came.

She got up, set the girl on the chair, and began to prepare the midday meal, hoping Phemy would help her and gain some comfort from activity. Nor was she disappointed. With a childish air of abstraction, Phemy rose and began, as of old in the house, to busy herself, and Kirsty felt much relieved.

"But, oh," she said to herself, "the soreness o' that wee heart i' the inside o' her!"

Phemy never spoke, and went about her work mechanically. When at length Mrs. Barclay came into the kitchen, Kirsty thought it better to leave them together, and went to find Steenie. She spent the rest of the day with him. Neither said a word about Phemy, but Steenie's countenance shone all the afternoon; and she left him at night in his house on the Horn, still in the afterglow of the meditation which had irradiated him in the morning.

When she came home, Kirsty found that her mother had put Phemy to bed. The poor child had scarcely spoken all day, and seemed to have no life in her. In the evening an attack of shivering, with other symptoms, showed that she was physically ill. Mrs. Barclay had sent for her father, but the girl was asleep when he came. Aware that he would not hear a word casting doubt on his daughter's discretion, and fearing that if she told him how she came to be there he would take her home at any risk, she had told him nothing of what had taken place, for Phemy would not be so well cared for at home as at the Knowe. He, thinking her ailment would prove but a bad cold, had gone back to his books without seeing her. At Mrs. Barclay's entreaty he had promised to send the doctor, but he forgot, and never thought of it again.

Kirsty found her very feverish, breathing with difficulty, and in considerable pain. She sat by her through the night. She had seen nothing of illness, but sympathetic insight is the first essential endowment of a good nurse.

All night long Steenie was roving within sight of the window where the light was burning. He did not know that Phemy was ill; pity for her heartache drew him thither. As soon as he thought his sister would be up, he went in. She heard him, and came to him. The moment he learned of Phemy's condition, he said he would go for the doctor. Kirsty in vain begged him to have some breakfast first, but he took a piece of oatcake in his hand and went.

The doctor returned with him, and pronounced the attack pleurisy. Phemy did not seem to care what became of her. She was ill a long time, and for a fortnight the doctor came every day.

There was now so much to be done that Kirsty could seldom go with Steenie to the hill. Nor did Steenie himself care to go for any time, and was never a night away from the house. When all were in bed, he would generally coil himself on a bench by the kitchen fire, at any moment ready to answer the lightest call of Kirsty, who took pains to make him feel useful, as indeed he was. Although now he slept considerably better at night and less in the day, he would start to his feet at the slightest sound, like the dog he had almost ceased to imagine himself except in his dreams. In carrying messages, or in following directions, he had always shown himself perfectly trustworthy.

Slowly, very slowly, Phemy recovered. But long before she was well, the family saw that the change for the better, which had been evident in Steenie's mental condition for some time before Phemy's illness, was now manifesting itself plainly in his person. His eyes appeared to shine less from his brain, and more from his mind; he stood more erect; and he had grown more naturally conscious of his body and its requirements. Kirsty, coming upon him one morning as he somewhat ruefully regarded his trousers, suggested a new suit, and was delighted to see his face shine up, and hear him declare himself ready to go with her and be measured for it. She found also soon after, to her joy, that he had for some time been enlarging with hammer and chisel a certain cavity in one of the rocks inside his house on the Horn, that he might use it for a bath.

In all these things she saw evident signs of a new start in the growth of his spiritual nature; and if she spied danger ahead, she knew that the God whose presence in him was making him grow, was ahead with the danger also.

Steenie not only now went attired as befitted David Barclay's son, but to an ordinary glance, would have appeared nowise remarkable. Kirsty ceased to look upon him with the pity hitherto coloring all her devotion; pride had taken its place, which she buttressed with a massive hope, for Kirsty was a splendid hoper. People in the town, where now he was oftener seen, would remark on the wonderful change in him.

Before long, Kirsty began to teach him to sit on a horse; and, after but a few weeks of her training, he could ride pretty well.

It was many weeks before Phemy was fit to go home. Her father came to see her now and then, but not very often; he had his duties to attend to, and his books consoled him.

As soon as Phemy was able to leave her room, Steenie constituted himself her slave, and was ever within her call. He seemed always to know when she would prefer having him in sight, and when she would rather be alone. He would sit for an hour at the other end of the room, and watch her like a dog without moving. He could have sat so all day; but, as soon as she was able to move about, nothing could keep Phemy in one place more than an hour at the utmost. By this time Steenie could read a little, and his reading was by no means as fruitless as it was slow; he would sit reading, nor at all lose his labor that, every other moment when within sight of her, he would look up to see if she wanted anything. To this mute attendance of love the girl became so accustomed that she regarded it as her right, nor had ever the spoiled little creature occasion to imagine that it was not yielded her; and if at a rare moment she threw him a glance or a small smile—a crumb from her table to her dog—Steenie would for one joyous instant see into the seventh heaven and all the day after dwell in the fifth or sixth. On fine clear noontides she would walk a little way with him and Snootie, and then he would talk to her as he had never done except to Kirsty, telling her wonderful things about the dog and the sheep, the stars and the night, and the clouds and the moon. But he never spoke to her of the Bonny Man. When, on their return, she would say they had had a pleasant walk together, his delight would be unutterable; but all the time Steenie had not once ventured a word belonging to any of the deeper thoughts in which his heart was most at home. Was it that in his own eyes he was but a worm glorified with the boon of serving an angel? Was it that he felt as if she knew everything of that kind, and he had nothing to tell her but the things that entered at his eyes and ears? Or was it that a sacred instinct of her incapacity for holy things kept him silent concerning such? At times he would look terribly sad, and the mood would last for hours.

Not once since she began to get better had Phemy alluded to her faithless lover. In its departure her illness seemed to have carried with it her unwholesome love for him; and certainly, as if overjoyed at her deliverance, she had become much more of a child. Kirsty was glad for her sake, and gladder still that Francie Gordon had done her no irreparable injury. As her strength returned, she regained the childish merriment which had always drawn Kirsty, and the more strongly that she was not herself lighthearted. Kirsty's rare laugh was indeed a merry one, but when happiest of all she hardly smiled. Perhaps she never would laugh her own laugh until she opened her eyes in heaven! But how can anyone laugh his real best laugh before that?

Phemy seemed more pleased to see her father every time he came, and Kirsty began to hope she would tell him the trouble she had gone through. But then Kirsty had a perfect faith in her father, and a girl like Phemy never has! Her father had never been father enough to her. He had been invariably kind and trusting, but his books had been more to his hourly life than his daughter. He had never drawn her to him, never given her opportunity of coming really near him.

CHAPTER TWENTY-ONE

Phemy Yields Place

It was a bright day in the last week of November when the doctor came himself to take Phemy home to her father. A thin carpet of snow lay on the ground, beneath which the roads were in good condition.

Mrs. Barclay and Kirsty busied themselves about Phemy, who was as playful and teasing as a pet kitten while they dressed her; but Steenie stayed in the darkest corner, watching everything, but offering no unneeded help. Without once looking or asking for him, Phemy climbed into the gig beside the doctor, began talking to him at once, and never turned her head as they drove away. The moment Steenie heard the sound of the horses' hoofs, he came quietly from the gloom and went out of the back door, thinking no eye was upon him. But his sister's heart was never off him, and her eyes were on him far more than he knew.

Of late he had begun again to go to the hill at night, and Kirsty feared his old trouble might be returning. Glad as she was to serve Phemy, she was far from regretting her departure, for now she would have leisure for Steenie and her books, and now the family would once again gather itself into the perfect sphere to which drop and ocean alike desires to shape itself!

"I thought ye would be after me!" cried Steenie, as she opened the door of his burrow, within an hour of his leaving the house.

Never doubting she would follow, he had already built up a good peat fire on the hearth, and beside it, he placed for her a low settle which his father had made for him, and he had himself covered with a sheepskin of thickest fleece. They sat silent for a while.

Kirsty had expected to find him full of grief because of Phemy's going, especially as the heartless girl never said good-bye to her most loving slave. Kirsty could certainly see on his countenance traces of emotion, and in his eyes the lingering trouble as of a storm all but overblown. There was, however, in his face the light as of a far sunk aurora, the outmost rim of whose radiance, seemed to encircle his whole person!

"Would ye say noo, Kirsty, that I was any use til her?" he asked at length.

"Jist a heap," answered Kirsty. "I kenna whatever she or I would have done wantin ye! She needed a heap o' lookin til!"

"And ye think mebbe she'll be some better, some way or ither, for 't?"

"Ay, I do think that, Steenie. But to tell the truth, I'm no sure she'll think verra often aboot what ye did for her!"

"Ow, na! What for should she? There's no need for that! It was for herself, no for her think-aboot-it I tried. I was jist fain to do somethin. When I came in that day—the day after ye brought her hame, ye ken—the look of her poor, bonny, sad face jist turned my heart over i' the midst o' me. I think, if I hadna been able to do anythin for her afore she went, I would have come hame here to my own hoose like a dyin sheep, and lain doon. Yon face o' hers comes back til me noo like the face o' a lost lammie that the shepherd didna think worth goin oot to look for. But if I had sic a sore heart for her, the Bonny Man must have had a sorer, and He'll do for her what He can—and that must be muckle—muckle! They call Him the Guid Shepherd, ye ken!"

He sat silent for some minutes, and Kirsty's heart was too full to let her speak. She could only say to herself, "And folk calls him half-witted, do they! Weel, let them! If he be half-witted, the Lord's made up the other half wi' better!"

"Ay!" resumed Steenie. "The Guid Shepherd loses no one o' them all! But I'll miss her dreadful! Eh, but I liked to watch her wan bit face grow and grow till i' was round and rosy again! And, eh, sic a bonny red and white as it was! And better yet I liked to see yon heartbreakin look o' the lost one wearin all away till 't was clean gone! And noo she's back til her father, bright and bonny as the lone starry night! Eh, but it makes me happy to think o' 't!"

"So it makes me!" responded Kirsty, feeling, as she regarded him, like a glorified mother beholding her child walking in the truth.

"And noo," continued Steenie, "I'm right glad she's gone, and my mind'll be more at ease—I tell ye what for. I must always tell you anythin that'll bide tellin, Kirsty, ye ken! Weel, a week or twa ago, I began to be troubled as I never was troubled afore. I canna weel say what was the cause o' 't, of the kind o' thing it was, but somethin had come that I didna want to come. Maybe ye'll ken what it was like when I tell ye that I was always think-thinkin aboot Phemy. Noo, afore she came, I was most always thinkin aboot the Bonny Man. It wasna that there was any sic necessity for thinkin aboot Phemy, for by that time she was oot o' her meesery, whatever that was. Afore her, when my mind would grow a bit quiet, and the powers o' darkness would draw themselves away a bit, always would come the face o' the Bonny Man, and fill me fresh up wi' the hope o' seein Him or long. But noo, at every moment, up would come, no the face o' the Bonny Man, but the face of Phemy, and I didna like that, and I couldna help it. And a scratchin fear gripped me, that I was turnin false to the Bonny Man. It wasna that I thought He would be vexed wi' me, but that I couldna bide anythin to come atween me and Him. I took myself weel over the heckles, but I couldna make oot that I could help it. No bein made like other fowk, I couldna think aboot twa things at once. But, as I say, it troubled me.

"Weel, the day, my heart was sore at her goin away, for I had been long used to seein her every hour, and the wish i' my heart at the time was to do somethin for her, and I clean forgot the Bonny Man! When she got intil the doctor's gig and away they drove, my heart grew cold. I was like one dead and beginnin to rot i' the grave. But that minute I heard, or it was jist as if I heard i' my heart, ye ken—a voice cry, 'Steenie! Steenie' and I cried loud oot, 'Comin, Lord!' but I kenned weel enough that voice was inside o' me, and no i' my head, but i' my heart! So away at once I came to my closet here, and sat doon and hearkened i' my heart. Never a word came, but I grew quiet—eh, so quiet and content like, wi'oot anythin to make me so, but maybe that He was thinkin aboot me! And I'm quiet yet. And as soon's it's dark, I shall go oot and see whether the Bonny Man be anywhere aboot. There's nothin atween Him and me noo, for the moment I begin to think, it's Him that comes to be thought aboot, and no Phemy any more!"

"Steenie," said Kirsty, "it was the Bonny Man sent Phemy til ye—to give ye something to do for Him, to look after one o' His silly lambs."

"Ay," returned Steenie, "I ken she wasna wiselike, sic as you and my mither. She needed a heap o' lookin after, as ye said."

"And," Kirsty explained, "wi' havin to look after her, He kenned that the thoughts that troubled ye wouldna so weel win, and would learn to bide oot. Jist look at ye noo! See hoo ye have learned to look after yerself! Ye saw it couldna be agreeable to her to have ye aboot her no that weel washed, and wi' clothes ye didna keep tidy and clean! Since ever ye took to lookin after Phemy, I have had little trouble lookin after you!"

"I see't, Kirsty, I see 't! I never thought o' the thing afore! I might do a heap to make myself more like other fowk! I shall no forget, noo that I have gotten a grip o' the thing. Ye'll see, Kirsty!"

"That's my own Steenie!" answered Kirsty. "Maybe the Bonny Man couldna be always comin to ye Himself, havin ither fowk a heap to look til, and so sent Phemy to let ye ken what He would have o' ye. Noo that ye have begun, ye'll be growin more and more like other fowk."

"Eh, but ye fleg me! I may grow over like other fowk! I must away oot, Kirsty! I'm growing fleyt."

"What for, Steenie?" cried Kirsty, not a little frightened herself, and laying her hand on his arm. She feared his old trouble was returning in force.

" 'Cause other fowk never sees the Bonny Man, they tell me," he replied.

"That's their own fault," answered Kirsty. "They might all see Him if they would—or at least hear Him say they should see Him ere long."

"I'm no so sure that ever I did see Him, Kirsty! But I have as guid as seen Him, Kirsty! He was there! He helped me when the ill folk came to pull at me! Ye do think, though, Kirsty, that I'm bound to see Him some day?"

"I'm thinkin the hour's been already set for that same!" answered Kirsty.

"Kirsty," returned Steenie, not quite satisfied with her reply, "I'll go clean oot the wits I have, if ye tell me I'm never to see Him face to face!"

"Steenie," rejoined Kirsty solemnly, "I would go oot o' my wits myself if I didna believe that! I believe 't wi' all my heart, my bonny man."

"Weel, and that's all right! But ye mustna call me yer bonny man, Kirsty, for there's but one Bonny Man, and we're all brithers and sisters. He said it Himself!"

"That's very true, Steenie, but whiles ye're so like Him I canna help callin ye by His name."

"Dinna do 't again, Kirsty. I canna bide it. I'm no bonny! No but I would sore like to be bonny—bonny like Him, Kirsty! Did ye ever hear tell that He had a Father? I heard a man say that He had. Sic a Bonny Man that Father must be! Jist think o' His havin a Son like Him! David Barclay must be right sore disappointed wi' sic a son as me—an him sic a man as himself! What for is 't, Kirsty?"

"That'll be one o' the secrets the Bonny Man's goin to tell His ain fowk when He gets them hame wi' Him!"

"His ain fowk, Kirsty?"

"Ay, siclike's you and me. When we go hame, He'll tell us all aboot a heap o' things we would fain ken."

"His ain fowk. His ain fowk!" Steenie went on for a while

murmuring to himself at intervals. At last he said, "What makes them His ain fowk, Kirsty?"

"What makes me your fowk, Steenie?" she rejoined. "It's 'cause we have the same father and mither! The Bonny Man and you and me, we have all the same Father; that's what makes us His ain fowk! Ye see noo?"

"Ay, I see! I see!" responded Steenie, and again was silent. Kirsty thought he had plenty now to meditate upon.

"Are ye comin hame wi' me," she asked, "or are ye goin to bide, Steenie?"

"I'll gang hame wi' ye, if ye like, but I would raither bide the night," he answered. "I'll have jist this one night more oot upo' the hill, and in the morn I'll come til the hoose, and see if I can help my mither, or maybe my father. That's what the Bonny Man would like best, I'm sure."

Kirsty went home with a glad heart. Surely Steenie was now becoming, as he phrased it, "like ither fowk"!

"But the Lord's gowk's better nor the warld's prophet!" she said to herself.

CHAPTER TWENTY-TWO

The Horn

The beginning of the winter had been open and warm, and very little snow had fallen. This was much in Phemy's favor, and by the new year she was quite well. But she was no longer like her old self. She was quieter and less foolish. She had had a lesson in folly, and a long ministration of love, and knew now a trifle about both. She wrote nearly as much poetry, but it was not so silly as before, partly because her imagination had now something of fact to go upon, and poorest fact is better than mere fancy.

At Mrs. Bremner's request, Phemy had arranged to go with her to visit a distant relation living in a lonely cottage on the other side of the Horn—a woman too old ever to leave her home. The weather gave signs of breaking that day, but the heavy clouds on the horizon seemed no worse than had often shown themselves that winter, and as often passed away. The air was warm, the day bright, the earth dry, and Phemy and her aunt were in good spirits. They had planned to return early to Weelset, but agreed as they went that, the days being so short, Phemy should take the nearer path to Tiltowie over the Horn. By this arrangement, their visit ended, Mrs. Bremner's way lying along the back of the hill, and Phemy's over the nearer shoulder of it.

As they took leave of each other a little later than they had intended, Mrs. Bremner cast a glance at the gathering clouds and expressed her concern over Phemy being caught by rain or snow. She made Phemy promise to hurry, and to change her wet clothes as soon as she reached home.

They parted, but before Phemy reached the top of the hill, which she had to cross by a path no better than a sheep track, the wind had turned to the north, and was blowing keen. With gathering strength from the regions of everlasting ice, it brought with it a terrible cold so that in a few minutes the slight creature had to fight for every step she took. When at length she reached the top, which lay bare to the continuous torrent of fierce and fiercer rushes, her strength was all but exhausted. The wind brought up heavier and heavier snow clouds, and darkness with them; but before the snow even began to fall, Phemy was in worse straits than she had ever known. In a few minutes the tempest had blown all energy out of her, and she sat down where there was not a stone to shelter her. When she rose, afraid to sit longer, she could not tell in which direction to turn. She began to cry, and the wind, not heeding her tears, seemed determined to blow her away. Then came the snow, filling the wind faster and faster, until at length the frightful blasts had in them more bulk of blinding and dizzying snowflakes than of the air which drove them.

Kirsty always enjoyed the winter heartily. For one thing, it roused her poetic faculty far more than the summer. That very afternoon, leaving Steenie with his mother, she paid a visit to the weem and there, in the heart of the earth, made a little song.

Long before she had finished writing it, the world was dark outside. She had heard but little heeded the roaring of the wind over her. When she put her head up out of the earth, it seized her by the hair as if it would drag it off. It took her more than an hour to get home.

In the meantime Steenie had been growing restless. Coming wind often affected him so. He had been out with his father, who expected a storm, to see that all was snug about byres and stables. Now he had come in and was wandering about the house. The clouds had gathered thick, and the afternoon was very dark, but all was as yet still. He called his dog and Snootie lay down at his feet, ready for what might come. Steenie sat on a stool, with his head on his mother's knee, and for a while seemed lost in thought. Then without moving or looking up, he said, as if thinking aloud, "It must be fine fun up there i' the clouds afore the flakes begin to spread!"

"What mean ye by that, Steenie, my man?" asked his mother.

"They must be packed so close, like feathers in a featherbed! And when they let them all oot thegither, like holdin the bed i' their twa hands by the bottom corners. Eh me! If I could but get rid o' my feet, and go up to see!"

"What for yer feet, Steenie? Feet's verra useful kind o' things to creatures whether in fours or twas!"

"Ay, but mine's sic a weight! It's them that's aye holdin me doon! I would have been up and away long since if it hadna been for them!"

"Where on earth get ye sic notions aboot yer feet? God kens there's nothin amiss wi' yer feet! Neither has ye any reason to be ashamed o' them. The fact is, *your* feet's ordinary small, Steenie, and can add but little to yer weight!"

"It's all that ye ken, mother!" answered Steenie with a smile. "But the Bonny Man Himself told the minister that told me, once I was at the kirk wi' you, mother—long, long since—twa or three hun'erd years, it seems. The Bonny Man told His ain fowk first that He was goin away so that they mightna be able to do wantin Him, and want to stir themselves and come up after Him. And so He slipped off His feet, and goed away up intil the air where the snow comes frae. And ever since He comes and goes as He likes. And after that He told the minister that we was to lay aside the weight that so easy besets us, and run. Noo by *run* He must have meaned *run up*, for a body's no to run frae the deevil but resist him; and what is 't that holds anybody frae runnin up the air but his feet? But He's promised to help me off wi' my feet some day. Think o' that! Eh, if I could get my feet off! Eh, if they would but stick i' my shoes, and go wi' them when I pull them off! They're nothin after all, ye ken, but the shoes o' soul!"

A gust of wind rose against the house, and sank as suddenly. "That'll be one o' them!" said Steenie, rising hastily. "He'll be wantin me. It's no that often they want anything o' me beyond the fair words all God's creatures look for frae one anither, but while they do want me, I must be goin!"

"Hoots, laddie!" returned his mother. "What can they be wantin o' siclike as you? Sit ye doon, and bide till they cry ye plain. I would fain have ye safe i' the hoose the night!"

"It's all His hoose, mither! All theroot's therein to Him. He's in His own hoose all the time, and I'm jist as safe atween His walls as atween yours. Didna nobody ever tell ye that, mither? Weel, I ken it to be true! And for wantin sic like as me, if God never has need o' a midge, what for does He make sic a lot o' them?"

" 'Deed it's true enough ye say!" returned his mother. "But I do wonder ye're no fleyt!"

"Fleyt!" rejoined Steenie. "What is there to be fleyt at? I never was fleyt at face o' man or woman—na, nor o' beast naither!"

"Noo hearken to me. Ye mustna go the night!" said his mother anxiously. "If yer father and Kirsty would but come in to persuade ye! I'm clean lost wi'oot them!"

"For the puir idiot hasna the sense to ken what's wanted o' him!" supplemented Steenie, with a laugh almost merry.

"Dare ye," cried his mother indignantly, "hint at sic a word and my bairn thegither? He's my bonny man!"

"Na, mither, na! *He's* the Bonny Man at whose feet I shall one day sit, clothed and i' my right mind, He *is* the Bonny Man!"

"Thank the Lord," continued his mother, still harping on the same outrage of such as called her child an idiot, "that ye're no an orphan—that there's three o' us to take yer part!"

"Nobody can be an orphan," said Steenie, "so long's God's no dead."

"And they call ye an idiot, do they!" exclaimed Marion Barclay. "Weel, be ye or no, ye're one o' the babes in whose mouth He perfecteth praise. But, eh, Steenie," she pursued, "ye willna go the night!"

"Mither," he answered, "ye dinna ken, nor do I yet, what to make o' me—what wits I have, and what wits I havena, but this ye'll allow, that, for anything ye ken the Bonny Man may be cryin upo' me to go after some puir little yowie o' His, oot i' the storm the night!" And with these words he walked gently from the kitchen, his dog following him.

A terrible blast rushed right into the fire when he opened the door. But he shut it behind him easily, and his mother comforted herself that she had known him out in worse weather. Kirsty entered a moment after, and when her father came in from his workshop, they had their tea, and sat peacefully round the fire talking, a little troubled but nowise uneasy that their Steenie, the darling of them all, was away on the Horn. He knew every foot of its sides better than the collie who was following at his master's heel.

The wind, which had fallen after the second gust as after the first snow, now began to blow with gathering force, and it took Steenie much longer than usual to make his way over height and hollow from his father's house to his own. But he was in no hurry, not knowing where he was wanted.

Before the snow had begun to fall, man and dog reached their refuge among the rocks, strong-toiling against the wind, and the night seemed solid with blackness. The very flakes might have been black as the snow of hell for any gleam they gave. But they arrived at last, and Steenie, making Snootie go in before him, entered the low door with bent head, and closed it behind him. The dog lay down wearily, but Steenie set about lighting the peats already piled between the great stones of the hearth. The wind howled over the waste hill in multitudinous whirls, and swept like a level cataract over the ghostly bog at its foot, but scarce a puff blew against the door of their burrow.

When his fire was well alight, Steenie seated himself by it on the sheepskin settle, and fell into a reverie. How long he had sat thus he did not know, when suddenly the wind fell, and with the lull master and dog started together to their feet. Was it a cry they heard, or but a moan between wind and mountain? The dog flew to the door with a whine and began to sniff and scratch at the crack of the threshold. Steenie reached for the lantern which he had never yet had occasion to use. The dog ran back to him and began jumping upon him, indicating thus that he wanted Steenie to open the door. A moment more and they were in the open universe, in a night all of snow, lighted by the wide swooning gleam of a hidden moon whose radiance, almost absorbed, came filtering through miles of snow cloud to reach the world. Nothing but snow was to be seen in heaven or earth, but for the present no more was falling. Steenie set the lighted lantern by the door and followed Snootie, who went sniffing and snuffling about.

Steenie always regarded animals, and especially dogs, as a lower sort of angels, with ways of their own. It was in part his intense desire to enter into the thoughts of his dog, that used to make him imitate him most of the day.

As the dog seemed to have no scent of anything, Steenie, after considering for a moment what he must do, began to walk in a spiral, beginning from the door, with the house for the center. He had gotten out of the little valley on to the open hill, and the wind had begun to threaten reawaking, when Snootie, who was a little way to one side of him, stopped short and began scratching like a fury in the snow. Steenie ran to him and dropped on his knees to help him—the dog had already got a part of something clear! It was a woman's arm! So deep was the snow over her that the cry he and the dog had heard could not have been uttered by her! He was gently clearing the snow from the head, and the snowlike features were vaguely emerging, when the wind gave a wild howl, the night·grew dark again, and in bellowing blackness the death-silent snow was upon them. But in a moment or two more, with Snootie's vigorous aid, he had drawn the body of a slight, delicately formed woman out of its cold, white mound. Somehow, with difficulty, he got it on his back, the only way he could carry it, and staggered away with it toward his house.

The body grew heavy on poor Steenie's back, and the cold out of it came through to his spine. His breathing grew very short, compelling him, several times, to stop and rest. His legs became insensible under him, and his feet got heavier and heavier in the snow-filled, entangling, impeding heather.

What if it were Phemy, he thought as he struggled on. But no, this was a dead thing, he feared—only a thing, no woman at all. Of course it couldn't be Phemy. She was at home, asleep in her father's house. He had always shrunk from death—even a dead mouse he could not touch without a shudder. But this was a woman and might come alive! It belonged to the Bonny Man, anyhow, and he would stay out with it all night, rather than have it lie there in the snow! He would not be afraid of her—he was nearly dead himself, and the dead were not afraid of the dead. She had only put off her shoes. But she might be alive, and he must get her into the house. He would like to put off his feet, but most people would rather keep them on, and he must try to keep hers on for her!

With fast failing energy he reached the door, staggered in, dropped his burden gently on his own soft heatherbed, and fell exhausted.

He lay but a moment, came to himself, rose, and looked at the lovely thing. It lay just as it had fallen from his back, its face uppermost. It *was* Phemy!

For a moment his blood seemed to stand still, and then all the divine sense of the half-witted returned to him. There was no time to be sorrowful over her—he must save the life that might yet be in that frozen form! He had nothing in the house except warmth, but more than anything else warmth was what the cold thing needed! With trembling hands he took off her half-thawed cloak, laid her in the thick blankets of his bed, and covered her with every woolen thing in the hut. Then he made up a large fire, in the hope that some of its heat might find her.

She showed no sign of life. Her eyes were fast shut. Not a trace of suffering was to be seen on her countenance. Death alone, pure, calm, cold, and sweet, was there. But Steenie had never seen death, and there was room for him to doubt and hope. He laid one fold of a blanket over the lovely white face, as he had seen a mother do with a sleeping infant; then he called

Snootie, and making him lie down on her feet, told him to watch. Then turning away, he went to the door. As he passed the fire, he coughed and grew faint, but recovering himself, picked up his fallen stick, and set out for Corbyknowe and Kirsty. Once more the wind had ceased, but the snow was yet falling.

CHAPTER TWENTY-THREE

The Storm Again

Kirsty woke suddenly out of a deep, dreamless sleep. A white face was bending over her—Steenie's—whiter than ever Kirsty had seen it. He was panting, and his eyes were huge. She started up.

"Come, come!" was all he was able to say.

"What's the matter, Steenie?" she gasped.

For a minute he stood panting, unable to speak.

"I'm no thinkin anythin's wrong," he faltered at length with an effort, recovering breath and speech a little. "The Bonny Man—"

He burst into tears and turned away. A vision of the white, lovely, motionless thing, whose hand had fallen from his like a lump of lead, lying alone at the top of the Horn, with the dog at her feet, had overwhelmed him suddenly.

Kirsty was sore distressed. She dreaded the worst when she saw him lose the self-restraint which had always been so remarkable in him. She leaned from her bed, threw her arms around him, and drew him to her. He kneeled, laid his head down, and wept as she had never known him weep.

"I'll take care o' ye, Steenie, my man!" she murmured. "Fear ye nothin."

It is amazing how much love will dare to promise in the strength of its own divinity.

"Ay, Kirsty, I ken ye will, but it's no me!" said Steenie. And he gave a brief, lucid account of what had occurred in the night.

"And noo that I have telled ye," he added, "it looks all so strange that maybe I have been but dreamin, after all! But it must be true, for that must have been what the angels came cryin upo' me for."

Kirsty told him to go and rouse the kitchen fire, and she would be with him in a minute. She sprang out of bed, and dressed as fast as she could, thinking what she had best take with her to help Phemy, but in her heart she had little hope. It would be a sad day for the schoolmaster.

She went to her parents' room, found them awake, and told them Steenie's tale.

"Ye must be off, lassie," said Marion, getting out of bed. "Take a wee whiskey wi' ye, but mind it's no that safe wi' frozen fowk. Hot milk's the best thing. Take a drappie o' that wi' ye. I shall be after ye wi' more. And dinna forget a piece to uphold ye as ye go. Dinna let Steenie go back wi' ye—he canna be fit. Send him to me, and I'll persuade him. David, my man," she said to her husband who was already rising, "ye'll have to saddle and ride. The doctor must go wi' ye straight to Steenie's hoose."

Kirsty went to heat some milk, but when she reached the kitchen, Steenie was not there, and the fire which he had tried to wake up, was all but black. The outer door was open, and the snow was drifting in. Steenie was gone into the storm again! She hurriedly poured some milk into a small bottle, and thrust it against her body to grow warm as she went. She lit the lantern, and set out.

She started running, certain, she thought, to overtake Steenie. The wind was up again, but it was almost behind her, and the night was not absolutely dark, for the moon was somewhere. She was far stronger than Steenie, and could walk faster; but keen as was her outlook on all sides, for the snow was falling too thick to let her see a little way through it, she reached the top of the Horn without seeing him. Had he dropped on the way? Had she in her haste left him after all in the house? One thing was sure—he could not have reached his house before her!

As she drew near the door she heard a short howl, and knew it for Snootie's. Perhaps Phemy had revived! But no, it was a desolate, forsaken cry! With a steady hand and prepared heart, she opened the door and went in. Snootie came bounding to her. Either he counted himself relieved, or could bear it no longer. He cringed at her feet, then leaped upon her; he saw in her his savior from the terrible silence and cold and motionless. Then he stood still before her, looking up to her, and wagging his tail, but his face plainly said, "It is there!"

Kirsty hesitated a moment. A weary sense of uselessness had overtaken her, and she shrank from encountering the unchanging and unchangeable. But she cast off the oppression, and followed the dog to the bedside. He jumped up, and lay down where his master had placed him, as if to say he knew his duty, had been lying there all the time, and had only got up the moment she came. It was the one warm spot in all the woolen pile. The feet beneath it were cold as the snow outside, and the lovely form lay motionless as a thing that would never move again. Kirsty lifted the blanket—there was Phemy's face, blind with the white death!

Hopeless, Kirsty yet tried her best to wake her from her snow-sleep, shrinking from nothing, except for the despair of it. But long ere she gave up the useless task, she was thinking far more about Steenie than Phemy.

"He did not come! He must be safe with his mother!" she kept saying in her heart, but she could not reassure herself. The forsaken fire, the open door haunted her. She would succeed for a moment or two in quieting her fears, calling them foolish, and the next they would rush upon her like a cataract, almost overwhelming her. While she was busy with the dead, he might be slowly sinking into the sleep from which she could not wake Phemy!

She laid the cold snow-captive straight, and left her to sleep on. Then, calling the dog, she left the hut in the hope of meeting her mother, and learning that Steenie was at home.

Now and then, while at her sad task, she had been reminded of the wind by its hollow roaring all about the hill; but not until she opened the door had she any notion how the snow was falling. And not until she left the hollow for the bare hillside did she realize how the wind was raging. Then indeed the world looked dangerous! If Steenie was out, if her mother had started, they were lost! She would have gone back to the hut with the dead, but that she might get home in time to prevent her mother from setting out, or might meet her on the way. At the same time the tempest between her and her home looked but a little less terrible to her than a sea breaking on a rocky shore.

CHAPTER TWENTY-FOUR

How Kirsty Fared

It was quite dark, and round her swept the whirlpool of snow. The swift flakes struck at her eyes and ears like a swarm of vicious flies. In such a wind, the blows of the soft thin snow, beating upon her face, now from one quarter, now from another, were enough to bewilder even a strong woman like Kirsty. After trying for a while to force her way, she suddenly became aware of utter ignorance as to the direction in which she was going and, for the first time in her life, a terror possessed her—not for herself, but for Steenie and her father and mother. To herself, Kirsty was nobody, but she belonged to David and Marion Barclay, and what were they and Steenie to do without her! They would go on looking for her till they too died and were buried yards deep in the snow!

She kept struggling on, her head bent, and her body leaning forward, forcing herself against the snow-filled wind. It was only by the feel of the earth under her feet, that she could tell where she was going, and at times she was by no means sure, whether she was going up or down hill. She kept on and on, almost hopeless of getting anywhere, certain of nothing but that if she once sat down, she would never rise again. Fatigue that must not yield, and the inroads of the cold sleep, at length affected her brain, and her imagination began to take its own way with her.

All the time, she felt in her dim suffering as if not she but those at home suffered. She had deserted them in trouble, and do what she might she would never get back to them! She could, she thought, if she put forth the needful energy, but the last self-exhaustive effort never would come!

Where was Snootie? He had left her! She tried to call him, but the storm choked every sound in her throat. He would never have left her to save himself! He who makes the dogs must be at least as faithful as they! So she was not left comfortless!

Then she heard, or thought she heard the church bell, and that may have had something to do with the strange dream out of which she came gradually to herself.

In her dream she sat at the communion table in her own parish church, with many others, none of whom she knew. A man with piercing eyes went along the table, examining the faces of all to see if they were fit to partake. When he came to Kirsty, he looked at her for a moment sharply, then said, "That woman is dead. She has been in the snow all night. Lay her in the vault under the church." She rose to go because she was dead, and hands were laid upon her to guide her as she went. They brought her out of the church into the snow and wind, and turned away to leave her. But she remonstrated. "The man with the eyes," she said, "gave the order that I should be taken to the vault of the church!" "Very well," answered a voice, "there is the vault! Creep into it." She saw an opening in the ground, at the foot of the wall of the church, and getting down on her hands and knees, crept through it, and with difficulty got into the vault. There all was still. She heard the wind raving, but it sounded far off. She had been bewildered by the terrible beating of the snow-wind, but her own wandering was another's guiding! Beyond the turmoil of life and unutterably glad, she fell asleep, and the dream left her. In a little while, however, it came again.

She thought she was lying on the stone floor of the church vault, and wondered whether the examiner with the shining eyes might not have made a mistake—perhaps she was not so very dead! Perhaps she was not quite unfit to eat of the Bread of

Life after all! She moved herself a little, then tried to rise, but failed. She tried again and again and at last succeeded. All was dark around her, but something seemed present that was known to her—whether man, woman, or beast, or thing, she could not tell. At last she recognized it. It was a familiar odor, a peculiar earthy smell—the air of her own earthhouse! Perhaps she was in it now! Then her box of matches might be there too! She felt about and found it. With trembling hands she struck one, and proceeded to light her lamp. It burned up, and something seized her by the heart.

A little farther in, stretched on the floor, lay a human form on its face. She knew at once that it was Steenie. The feet were toward her, and between her and them a pair of shoes. He was dead! He had got rid of his feet—he had gone after Phemy, gone to the Bonny Man! She knelt and turned the body over. Her heart was like a stone. She raised his head on her arm, and it was plain he was dead. A small stream of blood had flowed from his mouth, and made a little pool, not yet frozen. Kirsty's heart seemed about to break from her bosom to go after him, then the Eternal seemed to descend upon her like a waking sleep, a clear consciousness of peace. It was for a moment as if she saw the Father at the heart of the universe, with all His children about His knees. Her pain and sorrow and weakness were gone; she wept glad tears over the brother called so soon from the nursery to the great presence chamber.

"I wonder what God'll do wi' the twa!" she said to herself. "If I loved them both as I did, He loves them better! I *would* have died for them—and He *did!*" And she rose and went out.

Light had come at last, but too dim to be more than gray. The world was one large white sepulchre in which the earth lay dead. Warmth and hope and spring seemed gone forever. But God was alive. His hearthfire burned, and therefore death was nowhere! She knew it in her own soul, for the Father was there, and she knew that in His soul were all the loved. The wind had ceased, but the snow was still falling, here and there a flake. A faint blueness filled the air, and was colder than the white. Whether the day was at hand or the night, she could not distinguish. But Steenie was out of the snow—that was well! Or perhaps he was beside her in it, only he could leave it when he would! Surely anyhow Phemy must be with him! She could not be left all alone and she so silly! Steenie would have her to teach! His trouble must have gone the moment he died, but Phemy would have to find out what a goose she was! She would be very miserable, and would want Steenie! Kirsty's thoughts cut their own channels. She was as far ahead of her church as the woman of Samaria was ahead of the high priest at Jerusalem.

Thus thinking she kept on walking through the snow to weep on her mother's bosom. Suddenly she remembered and stood still—her mother was going to follow her to Steenie's house! She too must be dead in the snow! Well, let Heaven take all! They were born to die, and it was her turn now to follow her mother! She started again for home, and at length drew near the house.

It was more like a tomb than a house. The door looked as if no one had gone in or out of there for ages. Had she slept in the snow like the seven sleepers in the cave? Were the need and the use of houses and doors long over? Or was she a ghost come to have one more look at her old home in a long dead world? Perhaps her father and mother might have come back with like purpose, and she would see and speak to them! Or was she only in a dream, in which the dead would not speak to her? But God was not dead, and while God lived she was not alone, even in a dream!

A dark bundle lay on the doorstep—it was Snootie. He had been scratching and whining until despair came upon him, and he lay down prepared to die.

She lifted the latch, stepped over the dog, and entered. The peat fire was smoldering low on the hearth. She sat down and closed her eyes. When she opened them, there lay Snootie, stretched out before the fire! She rose, fed and roused the fire, and brought the dog some milk, which he lapped up eagerly.

Not a sound was in the house. She went all over it. Neither father nor mother was there. It was Sunday, and all the men were away. A cow lowed, and in her heart Kirsty blessed her— she was a live creature! She would go and milk her!

CHAPTER TWENTY-FIVE

How David Fared

The moment Kirsty had left the room, after telling them Steenie's tale, David Barclay dressed himself in haste, swallowed a glass of whiskey, saddled the gray mare, gave her a feed of oats, and set out for Tiltowie to get the doctor. Threatening as the weather was, he was well on the road before the wind became so full of snow as to cause him any anxiety, either for those on the hill or for himself. But after the first moment of anxiety, a very few minutes convinced him that a battle was at hand with the elements, more dangerous than any he had ever had to fight with armed men. For some distance the road was safe enough as yet, for the storm had not had time to heap up the snow between the bordering hills. But by and by, he must come out upon a wide track bordered by a bog, and be exposed to the full force of the now furious wind. When he reached the open, he was compelled to go at a footpace through the thick, blinding, bewildering tempest-driven snow. In spite of all his caution, he found, by the sudden sinking and withdrawing of one of his mare's legs with a squelching noise, that he had got astray upon the bog, nor knew in what direction the town lay. The only thing he did know was the side of the road to which he had turned, and that he knew only by the ground into which he had got; no step farther in that direction must be attempted. His mare seemed to know this as well as himself, for when she had pulled her leg out, she drew back a pace to stand on solid ground. David cast a knot on the reins, threw them on her neck, and told her to go where she pleased. She turned half round and started at once, feeling her way at first very carefully. Then she walked slowly on, with her head hanging low. Again and again she stopped and snuffed, diverged a little, and went on.

The wind was packed rather than charged with snow. Men said later that there never was a wind of this strength with so much snow in it. David began to despair of ever finding the road again, and naturally in such strait thought how much worse Kirsty and Steenie would be faring on the open hillside. His wife, he knew, could not have started before the storm rose to tempest, and would delay her departure. Then came the reflection, how little at any time a father could do for the well-being of his children! The fact of their being children implied their need of an all-powerful father—must there not then be such a father? Therewith the truth dawned upon him, that first of truths which all his churchgoing and Bible-reading had hitherto failed to disclose, that, for life to be a good thing and worth living, a man must be the child of a perfect Father and know Him. In his terrible perturbation about his children, he lifted up his heart— not to the Governor of the world, not to the God of Abraham or Moses, not in the least to the God of the Kirk, but to the faithful Creator and Father of David Barclay. The aching soul which none but a perfect Father could have created, capable of deploring its own fatherly imperfection, cried out to the Father of fathers on behalf of his children; and as he cried, a peace came stealing over him such as he had never before felt.

Then he knew that his mare had been for some time on hard ground, and was going with purpose in her gentle trot. In five minutes more, he saw the glimmer of a light through the snow. Near as it was, he failed repeatedly in finding his way to it. The mare at length fell over a stone wall out of sight in the snow, and when they got up they found themselves in a little garden at the end of a farmhouse. However, not until the farmer came to the door, wondering who on such a morning could be their visitor, did he know to what farm the mare had brought him. Weary, and well aware that no doctor in his senses would set out for the top of the Horn in such a tempest of black and white, he gratefully accepted the shelter and refreshment of which his mare and he stood in much need, and waited for a lull in the storm.

CHAPTER TWENTY-SIX

How Marion Fared

In the meantime the mother of the family, not herself at the moment in danger, began to suffer the most. It dismayed her to find that Steenie had, as she thought, insisted on accompanying Kirsty, but it was without any great anxiety that she set about preparing food with which to follow them.

She was bending over her fire, busy with her cooking when all at once the wind came rushing straight down the chimney, blew sleet into the kitchen, blew soot into the pot, and nearly put out the fire. It was but a small whirlwind, however, and presently passed.

She went to the door, opened it a little way, and peeped out. The morning was a chaos of blackness and snow and wind. She had been born and brought up in a yet wilder region, but the storm threatened to be such as in her experience was unparalleled.

"God preserve us!" cried the poor woman. "Can this be the end o' all things? Is the earth turnin intil a muckle snow wreath, that when all are dead, there may be no fowk left to bury them? Eh, mortal woman couldna carry a basket in sic a snowdrift! Losh, she wouldna carry herself far! I must bide a bit if I would be a help til them! It's my basket they'll be wantin, no me!"

She turned to her cooking as if it were the one thing to save the world. Let her be prepared for the best as well as for the worst! Kirsty might find Phemy past helping, and bring Steenie home! Then there was David, at that moment fighting for his life, perhaps. If he came home now, or any of the three, she must be ready to save their lives! They must not perish on her hands. So she prepared for the possible future, not by brooding on it, but by doing the work of the present. She cooked and cooked, until there was nothing more to be done in that way; and then, having thus cleared the way for it, she sat down and cried. There was a time for tears—the Bible said so—but not till Marion's fatigued hands fell into her lap was their hour come. To go out after Kirsty would have been the bare foolishness of suicide, would have been to abandon her husband and children against the hour of their coming need. One of the hardest demands on the obedience of faith is to do nothing. It is often so much easier to do foolishly!

But she did not weep long. A moment more and she was up and at work again, hanging a great kettle of water on the crook, and blowing up the fire, that she might have hot bottles to lay in every bed. Then she assailed the peat stack in spite of the wind, making journey after journey, until she had heaped a great pile of peats in the corner nearest the hearth.

The morning wore on, and the storm continued raging. No news came from the white world; mankind had vanished in the whirling snow. It was well the hired men had gone home, she thought. There would only have been the more in danger, the more to be fearful about, for all would have been abroad in the drift, hopelessly looking for one another! But oh, Steenie, and her own Kirsty!

About half-past ten o'clock the wind began to abate its violence, and speedily sank to a calm, wherewith the snow lost its main terror. She looked out. It was falling in straight, silent lines, flickering slowly down, but very thick. She could find her way now! Hideous fears assailed her, but she banished them imperiously. They should not sap the energy whose every jot would be wanted! She caught up the bottle of hot milk she had kept ready, wrapped it in flannel, tied it with a loaf of bread, in a shawl about her waist, made up the fire, closed the door, and set out for Steenie's house on the Horn.

CHAPTER TWENTY-SEVEN

Husband and Wife

Two hours or so earlier, David, perceiving some assuagement in the storm, and his host having offered to go at once to the doctor and the schoolmaster, had taken his mare and mounted to go home. He met with no impediment now except the depth of the snow, which made it hard for the mare to get along. Full of anxiety about his children, David found the distance a weary one to traverse.

When at length he reached the Knowe, no one was there to welcome him. But he saw by the fire and the food, that Marion was not long gone. He put up the mare, clothed and fed her, drank some milk, caught up some of the oatcakes, and started for the hill.

The snow was not falling so thickly now, but it had already almost obliterated the footprints of his wife. Still he could distinguish them in places, and with some difficulty succeeded in following their track until it was clear which route she had taken. They indicated the easier, though longer way—not that by the earthhouse—and so the father and daughter passed without seeing each other. When Kirsty got to the farm, her father was following her mother up the hill.

When David reached Steenie's house, he found the door open and walked in. His wife did not hear him, for his ironshod shoes

were balled with snow. She was standing over the body of
Phemy, looking down on the white sleep with a solemn, mother-
ly, tearless face. She turned as he drew near, and the pair, like
the lovers they were, fell each in the other's arms. Marion was
the first to speak.

"Eh, David! God be praised I have yerself!"

"Is the puir thing gone?" asked her husband in an awe-
hushed tone, looking down on the maid that seemed not dead
but sleeping.

"There's no doobt aboot that," answered Marion, "I was jist
thinkin that Steenie would be sore disappointed to learn that
there was. Eh, the faith o' that laddie! Heaven to him's sic a real
place, that he would not only fain be there himself, but would
have Phemy there—ay, if it were ever so long afore himself! Ye
see he kens nothin aboot sin and the sacrifice, and he doesna
understand that Phemy was aye a strong-willed kind o' lassie!"

"Maybe the Bonny Man, as Steenie calls Him," returned David, "may have as muckle compassion for the puir thing i' the
heart o' Him as Steenie himself!"

"Ow, ay! What for no! But what can the Bonny Man Himself
do?"

"Dinna limit the Almighty, woman. The Lord o' mercy'll
manage to look after the lammie He made, one way or ither,
there as here. Ye darena say He didna do His best for her here,
and will He no do His best for her there as weel?"

"Doobtless, David! But ye fright me! It sounds jist rank papist-
ry—neither more nor less! What can He do? He canna die again
for one that wouldna turn til 'im i' this life! The thing's no to be
thought!"

"Hoo ken ye that, woman? Ye have jist thought it yerself! If I
was you, I wouldna dare to say what He couldna do! I' the
meantime, what He makes me able to hope, I'm no goin to fling
frae me!"

David was a true man. He could not believe a thing with one
half of his mind, and care nothing about it with the other. He,
like his Steenie, believed in the Bonny Man about in the world,
not in the mere image of Him standing in the precious shrine of

the New Testament.

After a brief silence he asked, "Where's Kirsty and Steenie?"

"The Lord kens. I dinna."

"They'll be safe enough."

And therewith, by the side of the dead, he imparted to his wife the thoughts that drove misery from his heart as he sat on his mare in the storm with the reins on her neck, nor knew whither she went.

"Ay, ay," returned his wife after a pause. "Ye're right, David, as aye ye are. And I'm jist conscience-stricken to think that all my life long I have been ready to mourn over the sorrow i' my heart, never thinkin o' the gladness i' God's! What call had I to grieve over Steenie, when God must have been aye sore pleased wi' him! What sense is there in lamentation so long's God's evident settin all right! His heart's the safety o' oors. And eh, glad sure He must be, wi' sic a lot o' His bairns at hame aboot Him!"

"Ay," returned David with a sigh, thinking of his old comrade and the son he had left behind him, "but there's the prodigal ones!"

"Thank God, we have no prodigal!"

"Ay, thank Him!" rejoined David. "But He has prodigals that trouble Him sore, and we must see til 't that we no be thankless auld prodigals oorselves!"

Again followed a brief silence.

"Eh, but isna it strange?" said Marion. "Here's you and me mournin over anither man's bairn, and nowise kennin what's come o' oor ain twa! David, what can have come o' Steenie and Kirsty?"

"The will o' God's what's come o' them, and God hold me i' the grace o' wishin nothin ither nor that same!"

"Hold to that, David, and hold me til 't. We kenna what's comin!"

"The will o' God's comin," insisted David. "But eh," he added, "I'm concerned for puir Maister Craig!"

"Weel, let's away home and see whether the twa no be there afore us! Eh, but the sight o' Phemy must have given Steenie a sore heart! I wouldna wonder if he never get over 't i' this life!"

"But what'll we do aboot it? The storm may come on again worse nor ever, and make it impossible to bury her for a month!"

"We couldna carry her hame atween us, David—think ye?"

"Na, na, it's no as if it was herself! And cold's a fine keeper— better nor all the embalmin o' the Egyptians! Only I'm fain to keep Steenie from seein her again!"

"Weel, let's lay her i' the bonny white snow!" said Marion. "She'll keep there as long as the snow keeps, and nothin'll disturb her til the time comes to lay her away!"

"That's weel thought o'!" answered David. "Eh, woman, but it's a bonny burial compared wi' sic as I have often given comrade and foe alike!"

They went out and chose a spot close by the house where the snow lay deep. There they made a hollow, and pressed the bottom of it down hard. Then they carried out and laid in it the death-frozen dove, and heaped upon her a firm, white, marblelike tomb of heavenly new-fallen snow.

Without reentering it, they closed the door of Steenie's refuge, and leaving the two deserted houses side by side, made what slow haste they could, with anxious hearts, to their home. The snow was falling softly, for the wind was still asleep.

CHAPTER TWENTY-EIGHT

What Was Left

Kirsty saw their shadows darken the wall, and turning from her work at the dresser, ran to the door to meet them.

"God be thanked!" cried David.

Marion gave her daughter one loving look, and entering, cast a fearful, questioning glance around the kitchen.

"Where's Steenie?" she said.

"He's wi' Phemy, I'm thinkin," faltered Kirsty.

"Lassie, are ye demented?" her mother almost screamed. "We're this minute come frae there!"

"He is wi' Phemy, mither."

"Kirsty, I hold ye accoontable for my Steenie!" cried Marion, sinking on a chair, and covering her face with her hands.

"It's the will o' God that's accountable for him, woman!" answered David, sitting down beside her, and laying hold of her arm.

She burst into terrible weeping.

"He must be at hame wi' the Bonny Man!" said Kirsty.

"Lassie," said David, "you and me and your mither, we have nothin left but be better bairns, and go the faster to the Bonny Man! Where's what's left o' the laddie, Kirsty?"

"Lyin i' my hoose, as he called it. He was away afore I went to the kitchen. He had jist killed himself savin Phemy, runnin, upo' the barest chance o' savin her life, and so when he set off again to go til her, no bidin for me, he must ha' had a blood-break in 'is breast, and was jist able, and no more, to creep intil the weem oot o' the snow. He didna like the place, and yet had a kind o' a notion o' the Bonny Man bein there. I'm thinkin Snootie must have went til him, and run hame for help, for I found him a'most dead upo' the doorstep."

David stooped and patted the dog.

"Na, that couldna be," he said, "or he would never have left him, I'm thinkin. Ye're a brave dog!" he said to the collie. "But guid comes to guid doggies!" he added, fondling the creature, who had risen and feebly set his paws on his knee.

"And ye left him lyin there! Hoo had ye the heart, Kirsty?" sobbed the mother reproachfully.

"Mither, he was better off nor any ither one o' us! I willna say, mither, that I loved him so weel as ye loved him, and I darena say I loved him as the Bonny Man loves His brithers and sisters all. But the Bonny Man wanted him, and He has him! And when I left him there, it was jist as if I held him oot i' my arms and said, 'Here, Lord, take him: he's Yer ain!' "

"Ye're in the right, Kirsty, my bonny bairn!" said David. "Yer mither and me, we was never but pleased wi' anythin that ever ye did. Isna that true, Mar'on, my ain woman?"

"True as his word!" answered the mother, and rose and went to her room.

David sought the yard, saw that all was right with the beasts, and fed them. Then he made his way to his workshop over the cartshed, where in five minutes he constructed, with two poles run through two sacks, a very good stretcher, carrying it to the kitchen, where Kirsty sat motionless, looking into the fire.

"Kirsty," he said, "ye're a'most as strong's a man, and I wouldna have any but oor own three selves lay finger upo' what's left o' Steenie. Are ye up to takin the feet o' 'im to bring him hame? Here's what'll make it a'most easy!"

Kirsty rose at once. "A drappy o' milk, and I'm ready," she answered. "Will ye no take a mou'ful o' whiskey, father?"

"Na, na. I want nothin," replied David.

When he asked her to help him carry the body of her brother home through the snow, he had not yet learned what Kirsty went through the night before. Kirsty, however, knew no reason why she should not be as able as her father.

He took the stretcher, and they set out, saying nothing to the mother. She was still in her own room, and they hoped she might fall asleep.

"It reminds me o' the women goin til the sepulchre!" said David. "Eh, but it must have been a sore time til them—a heap sorer nor this heartbreak here!"

"Ye see they didna ken that He wasna dead," assented Kirsty, "and we do ken that Steenie's no dead! He's maybe walkin aboot wi' the Bonny Man—or maybe jist restin himself a wee after the uprisin! Just think o' his head bein alright! Eh, but Steenie must be in great glee!"

Thus talking as they went, they reached and entered the earth house. They found no angels on guard, for Steenie had not to get up again.

David wept the few tears of an old man over the son who had been of no use in the world but the best use—to love and be loved. Then, one at the head and the other at the feet, they brought the body out, and laid it on the bier.

Kirsty went in again and took Steenie's shoes, tying them in her apron.

"His feet's no sic a weight noo!" she said, as together they carried their burden home.

The mother met them at the door.

"Eh!" she cried. "I thought the Lord had taken ye both, and left me lone 'cause I was so hardhearted! But noo that He's brought ye back—and Steenie, what there is o' him, puir bairn—I shall never say anither word, but jist let Him do as He likes. There, Lord, I have done."

They carried the forsaken thing up the stair, and laid it on Kirsty's bed, looking so like and so unlike Steenie asleep. Marion was so exhausted, both mind and body, that her husband insisted on her postponing all further ministration till the following morning. But that night Kirsty unclothed the untenanted, and put on it a long white nightgown. When the mother saw it lying thus, she smiled and wept no more. She knew that the Bonny Man had taken home His idiot.

CHAPTER TWENTY-NINE

From Snow to Fire

This same winter, Francis Gordon was in India. It was the year of the mutiny, and his father's old regiment, in which he served, had lain for months besieged in a well-known city by the native troops. They had begun to know what privation meant. Danger and sickness, wounds and fatigue, hunger and death, had brought out the best that was in the worst of them; when their country knew how they had fought and endured, she was proud of them.

Francis Gordon had done his part, and well.

The effect of the punishment Kirsty had given him would be difficult to analyze, but its influence was upon him through the whole of the terrible time—none the less beneficent that his response to her stinging blows was indignant rage. Had she not defended herself so that he could not reach her, it cannot be speculated what he might have done in the first instinctive motions of natural fury. It is possible that only Kirsty's skill and courage saved him from what he would never have surmounted the shame of—taking revenge on a woman avenging a woman's wrong.

When he came to himself, the first bitterness of the incident over, he was convinced that the playmate of his childhood, whom once he loved best in the world, and who when a girl refused to marry him, had come to despise him, and for good reason. The idea took a firm hold on him, and became his most frequently recurring thought. The wale of Kirsty's whip served to recall it a good many days, and long after that had ceased either to smart or show, the thought would return in the night watches, and was certain to come when he had done anything his conscience called wrong, or his judgment foolish.

The officers of his mess were mostly men of character with ideas better at least than ordinary as to what became a man, and their influence on one by no means of a low, though of an unstable nature, was elevating. A change into a regiment of jolly, good-mannered, unprincipled men would within a month have brought him to do as they did, and in another month would have quite silenced his poor little conscience. After reaching India, events had been in his favor. He had no time to be idle. The mutiny broke out; he must bestir himself, and the best in him was called to the front.

He was specially capable of action with show in it. Let eyes be bent upon him, and he would go far. The presence of his kind to see and commend was an inspiration to him. Left to act for himself, undirected and unseen, his courage would not have proved of the highest order. Throughout the siege he was noted for a daring that often left the bounds of prudence far behind. More than once he was wounded—once seriously, but even then he was soon at his post again. His genial manners and friendly endurance rendered him a favorite with all.

The sufferings of the besieged at length grew such, and there was so little likelihood of the approaching army being able for some time to relieve the place, that orders were issued by the commander-in-chief to abandon it. Every British person must be out of the city before the night of the following day. The general in charge thereupon resolved to take advantage of the very bad watch kept by the enemy, and steal away in silence the same night.

The order was given to the companies, to each man individually, to prepare for the perilous attempt, but to keep it absolutely secret save from those who were to accompany them. So cautious was the little English colony, as well as the garrison, that not a rumor of the intended evacuation reached the besiegers; throughout the lines and in the cantonments, it was thoroughly understood that at a certain hour of the night, without call of bugle or beat of drum, everyone should be ready to march. Ten minutes after that hour the garrison was in motion. With difficulty, yet with sufficing silence, the gates were passed and the abandonment effected.

The first shot of the enemy's morning salutation, earlier than usual, went tearing through a bungalow within whose shattered walls lay Francis Gordon. In a dining room, whose balcony and window frame had been smashed the day before, he still slumbered wearily, when close past his head rushed the eighteen-pounder with its infernal scream. He started up, to find the blood flowing from a splinter wound on his temple and cheek-bone. A second shot struck the foot of his long chair. He sprang from it, and hurried into his coat and waistcoat.

But how was all so still inside? Not one gun answered! Firing at such an hour, he thought, the rebels must have got wind of their intended evacuation. It was too late for that, but why did not the garrison reply? Between the shots he seemed to hear the universal silence. Heavens! Were their guns already spiked? If so, all was lost! But it was daylight! He had overslept! He ought to have been with his men—how long ago he could not tell—for the first shot had taken his watch. A third came and broke his sword, carrying the hilt of it through the wall on which it hung. Not a sound, not a murmur reached him from the fortifications. Could the garrison be gone? Was the hour past? Had no one missed him? Certainly no one had called him! He rushed into the compound. Not a creature was there! He was alone—one English officer amid an army of hating Indians!

But they did not yet know that their prey had slid from their grasp, for they were going on with their usual gun reveille, instead of rushing on flank and rear of the retreating column! He might yet elude them and overtake the garrison! Half-dazed, he hurried for the gate by which they were to leave the city. Not a live thing save two starved dogs did he meet on his way. One of them ran from him. The other would have followed him, but a ball struck the ground between them, raising a cloud of dust, and he saw no more of the dog.

He found the gate open, and not one of the enemy in sight. Tokens of the retreat were plentiful, making the track he had to follow plain enough.

But now an enemy he had never encountered before—a sense of loneliness, desertion, and helplessness—all at once assailed him. He had never in his life congratulated himself on being alone—not that he loved his neighbor, but that he loved his neighbor's company, making him less aware of an uneasy self. And now first he realized that he had seen his sword hilt go off with a round shot, and had not caught up his revolver. He was absolutely unarmed.

He quickened his pace to overtake his comrades. On and on he trudged through nothing but rice fields, the day growing hotter and hotter, and his sense of desolation increasing. Two or three natives passing him looked at him, he thought, with sinister eyes. He had eaten no breakfast and was not likely to have any lunch. He grew sick and faint, but there was no refuge. He must walk until he fell and could walk no more! With the heat and his exertion, his hardly healed wound began to assert itself, and by and by he felt so ill that he turned off the road and lay down. While he lay, the eyes of his mind began to open to the fact that the courage he had hitherto been so eager to show could hardly have been of the right sort, seeing it was gone— evaporated clean away.

He rose and resumed his walk, but at every smallest sound started in fear of a lurking foe. With vainest regret he remembered the long-bladed dagger he had when a boy carried always in his pocket. It was exhaustion and illness, true, that destroyed his courage, but nonetheless was he a man of fear, nonetheless felt he a coward. Again he got into a ditch and lay down, in a minute or two again got up and went on, his fear growing until, mainly through consciousness of itself, it ripened into abject terror. Loneliness seemed to have taken the shape of a watching omnipresent enemy, out of whose diffusion death might at any moment break in some hideous form.

It was getting toward night when at length he saw dust ahead of him, and soon after, he could make out the straggling rear of the retreating English. Before he reached it a portion had halted for a little rest, and he was glad to lie down in a rough cart. Long before the morning the cart was on its way again, Gordon in it, raving with fever, and unable to tell who he was. He was soon in friendly shelter, however, under skillful treatment, and tenderly nursed.

When at length he seemed to have almost recovered his health, it was clear that he had in great measure lost his reason.

CHAPTER THIRTY

Kirsty Shows Resentment

Things were going from bad to worse at Castle Weelset. Whether Mrs. Gordon had disgusted her friends or grown tired of them was never known, but she remained at home and seldom had any visitors. Rumor, busy in country as in town, said she was more and more manifesting herself a slave to strong drink. She was tired of herself. She never read a book, never had a newspaper sent her, never inquired how things were going on about the place or in any part of the world, did nothing for herself or others, only ate, drank, slept, and raged at those around her.

One morning David Barclay, having occasion to see the factor, went to the castle, and finding he was at home ill, thought he would make an attempt to see Mrs. Gordon and offer what service he could render. She might not have forgotten that in old days he had been a good deal about the estate. She received him at once, but behaved in such an extraordinary fashion that he could not have any doubt she was at least half drunk. There was no sense either to be got out of her or put into her.

At Corbyknowe they heard nothing of the young laird. The papers said a good deal about the state of things in India, but Francis Gordon was not mentioned.

In the autumn of the year, when the days were growing short and the nights cold in the high region about the Horn, the son of a neighboring farmer, who had long desired to know Kirsty better, called at Corbyknowe with his sister, ostensibly on business with David. They were shown into the parlor, and all were sitting together in the early gloaming, the young woman bent on persuading Kirsty to pay them a visit and see the improvements they had made in house and garden, and the two farmers lamenting the affairs of the property on which they were tenants.

"But I hear there's a new grief like to come to the auld lairdship," said William Lammie, as he sat with an elbow on the tea table whence Kirsty was removing the crumbs.

"And what may the wisdom o' the countryside be puttin forth noo?" asked David in a tone of good-humored irony.

"Weel, as I hear, Mistress Comrie's been to Edinbro' for a week or twa, and has come hame wi' a queer story concernin the young laird—away oot there where there's been sic a rumpus wi' the heathen soldiers. There's word come, she says, that he's fallen intil the verra glare o' disgrace! And they had him afor a court martial, as they call 't. He'll have ill showin the face o' 'im again in 'is own country!"

"It's a lie," said Kirsty. "I shall take my oath o' that. There never was mark o' coward upo' Francie Gordon. He had his faults, but no one o' them looked that way. He was kind o' softlike whiles, and easy come over, but, havin little fear myself, I ken a coward when I see him. Somethin may have set up his pride—he has enough o' that for twa deevils—but Francie was never no coward!"

"Dinna lay the lie at my door. I beg o' ye, Miss Barclay. I was but tellin ye what fowk was sayin."

"Fowk's aye sayin, and seldom sayin true. The worst o' 't is that honest fowk's aye ready to believe liars! They dinna lie themselves, and so it's no easy to them to think anither would. Thereby the false word has free course and is glorified! They're no all liars that spreads the lie, but for them that makes the lie, the Lord silence them!"

"Hoots, Kirsty," said her mother, "it disna become ye to curse nobody! It's no right o' ye."

"It's a guid Bible curse, mither! It's but a way o' sayin, 'His will be done!' "

"Ye needna be so fell aboot the laird, Miss Barclay! He was no partic'lar friend o' yours if all tales be true!" remarked her admirer.

"I'm tellin ye tales is mostly lies. I have kenned the laird since he was a wee laddie, and I'm no goin to hear him lied upo' and hold my tongue! A lie's a lie whether the liar be a liar or no!" And she did not speak another word to him save to bid him good-night.

In the beginning of the new year, a rumor went about the country that the laird had been seen at the castle, but it died away. David pondered, but asked no questions, and Mrs. Bremner volunteered no information.

Kirsty of course heard the rumor, but she never took much interest in the goings on at the castle. Mrs. Gordon's doings were not such as the angels desire to look into, and Kirsty, not so distantly related to the angels, and inheriting a good many of their peculiarities, minded her own business.

CHAPTER THIRTY-ONE

A Race with Death

One night in January, when snow was falling thick, but the air, because of the cloud-blankets overhead, was not piercing, Kirsty went out to the workshop to tell her father that supper was ready. David was a Jack-of-all-trades, therein resembling a sailor rather than a soldier, and by the light of a single dip candle was busy with some bit of carpenter's work.

He did not raise his head when she entered, and heard her as if he did not hear. She wondered a little and waited. After a few minutes of silence, he said quietly, without looking up, "Are ye aware o' anythin by ordinary, Kirsty?"

"Na, nothin, father," answered Kirsty, wondering still.

"It's been bearin itself upo' me at my bench here, that Steenie's aboot the place the night. I canna help imaginin' he's been upo' this verra floor over and over again since I came oot, as if he would fain say something but couldna, and went away again."

"Think ye he's here at this moment, father?"

"Na, he's no."

"He used to think whiles the Bonny Man was aboot!" said Kirsty reflectively.

"My mother was a highland woman, and had the second sight. There was no manner o' doobt aboot it!" remarked David, also thoughtfully.

"And what would ye draw frae that, father?" asked Kirsty.

"Ow, nothin verra important, maybe, but just that possibly it might be i' the family!"

"I would like to ken yer verra thought, father."

"Weel, it's jist this: I'm thinkin some may be nearer the dead than ithers."

Kirsty turned her face toward the farthest corner. The place was rather large, and everywhere dark except within the narrow circle of the candlelight. In a quiet voice, with a little quaver in it, she said aloud, "If ye be here, Steenie, and have the power, let's ken if there be anythin lyin til oor hand that ye wish done. I'm sure, if there be, it's for oor sakes and no for yer own, glad as we would all be to do anythin for ye. The Bonny Man lets ye want for nothin—we're sure o' that!"

"Ay are we, Steenie," assented his father.

No voice came from the darkness. They stood silent for a while. Then David said, "Go in, lassie. Yer mother'll be wonderin what's come o' ye. I'll be in in a minute. I have jist the last stroke to give this bit jobby."

Without a word, but with disappointment in her heart that Steenie had not answered them, Kirsty obeyed. But she went round through the rickyard that she might have a moment's thought with herself. Not a hand was laid upon her out of the darkness, no faintest sound came to her ears through the silently falling snow. But as she took her way between two ricks, where was just room for her to pass, she felt without the slightest sense of material opposition, that she could not go through. Endeavoring afterward to describe what rather she was aware of than felt, she said the nearest she could come to it, was to say that she seemed to encounter the ghost of solidity. Certainly nothing seemed to touch her. She made no attempt to overcome the resistance, and the moment she turned, knew herself free to move in any other direction. But as the house was still her goal, she tried another space between two of the ricks. There again she found she could not pass. Making a third attempt in yet another interval, she was once more stopped in like fashion.

With that came the conviction that she was wanted elsewhere, and with it the thought of the Horn. She turned her face from the house and made straight for the hill, only that she took, as she had generally done with Steenie, the easier and rather longer way.

The notion of the presence of Steenie, which had been with her all the time, naturally suggested his house as the spot where she was wanted, and thither she sped. But the moment she reached, almost before she entered it, she felt as if it were utterly empty—as if it had not in it even air enough to give her breath.

Kirsty did not remain a moment in Steenie's house, but set her face to go home by the shorter and rougher path leading over the earthhouse and across the little burn.

The night continued dark, with an occasional thinning of the obscurity when some high current blew the clouds aside from a little nest of stars. Just as Kirsty reached the descent to the burn, the snow ceased, the clouds parted, and a faint worn moon appeared. She looked just like a little old lady too thin and too tired to go on living more than a night longer. But her waning life was yet potent over Kirsty, and her strange, wasted beauty, dying to rise again, made her glad as she went down the hill through the snowcrowned heather. The oppression which came on her in Steenie's house was gone entirely, and in the face of the pale ancient moon her heart grew so light that she broke into a silly song which, while they were yet children, she made for Steenie, who was never tired of listening to it:

Willy, wally, woo!
Hame comes the coo,
Hummle, bummle, moo!
Hame to fill the cogie!
Bonny hummle coo,
Wi' her baggy fu'
O' butter and o' milk,
And cream as soft as silk.
A'gathered frae the gerse
Intil her tassly purse,

> To be oors, no hers,
> Gudewillie, hummle, coo!
> Willy, wally, woo!
> Moo, Hummlie, moo!

Singing this childish rhyme, dear to the slow-waking soul of
Steenie, she had come almost to the bottom of the hill, was just
stepping over the top of the weem, when something like a groan
startled her. She stopped and sent a keen-searching glance
around. It came again, muffled and dull. It must be from the
earthhouse! Somebody was there! It could not be Steenie, for
why should Steenie groan? But he might be calling her, and the
weem changing the character of the sound! Anyhow she must
be wanted! She dived in.

She could scarcely light the candle, for the trembling of the
hand and the beating of her heart. Slowly the flame grew, and
the glimmer began to spread. She stood speechless, and stared.
Out of the darkness at her feet grew the form, as it seemed, of
Steenie, lying on his face, just as when she found him there a
year before. She dropped on her knees beside him.

He was alive, at least, for he moved! "Of course," thought
Kirsty, "he's alive. He never was anything else!" His face was
turned away from her, and his arm was under it. The arm next
to her lay out on the stones, and she took the ice-cold hand in
hers. It was not Steenie's! She took the candle and leaned across
to see the face. God in heaven! There was the mark of her
whip—it was Francie Gordon! She tried to rouse him but could
not. He was cold as ice, and seemed all but dead. But for the
groan she had heard, she would have been sure he was dead.
She blew out the light and, swift as her hands could move, took
garment after garment off herself, and laid them, warm from
her live heart, over and under him—all save one which she
thought too thin to do him any good. Last of all, she drew her
stockings over his hands and arms and, leaving her shoes where
Steenie's had lain, darted out of the cave. At the mouth of it she
rose erect like one escaped from the tomb, and sped in dim-
gleaming whiteness over the snow, scarce to have been seen

against it. The moon was but a shred—a withered autumn leaf low-fallen toward the dim plain of the west.

As she ran she would have seemed to one of Steenie's angels, out that night on the hill, a newly disembodied ghost fleeing home. Swift and shadowless as the thought of her own brave heart, she ran. Her sense of power and speed was glorious. She felt—not thought—herself a human goddess, the daughter of the Eternal. Up height and down hollow she flew, running her race with death, not an open eye, save the eyes of her father and mother, within miles of her in a world of sleep and snow and night.

Nor did she slacken her pace as she drew near the house, she only ran more softly. At last she threw the door to the wall, and shot up the steep stair to her room, calling her mother as she went.

CHAPTER THIRTY-TWO

Back from the Grave

When David came into supper, he said nothing, expecting Kirsty every moment to appear. Marion was the first to ask what had become of her. David answered she had left him in the workshop.

"Bless the bairn! What can she be aboot this time o' night?" said her mother.

"I kenna," returned David.

When they had sat eating their supper for ten minutes, vainly expecting her, David went out to look for her. Returning unsuccessful, he found that Marion had sought her all over the house with like result. Then they became uneasy.

Before going to look for her, however, David had begun to suspect her absence in one way or another connected with the subject of their conversation in the workshop, to which he had not for the moment meant to allude. When now he told his wife what had passed, he was a little surprised to find that immediately she grew calm.

"Ow, then, she'll be wi' Steenie!" she said.

Nor did her patience fail, but revived that of her husband. They could not, however, go to bed, but sat by the fire, saying a word or two now and then. The slow minutes passed, and neither of them moved save David once to put on peats.

The house door flew open suddenly, and they heard Kirsty cry, "Mither, mither!" but when they hastened to the door, no one was there. They heard the door of her room close, however, and Marion went up the stair. By the time she reached it, Kirsty was in a thick petticoat and buttoned-up cloth jacket, had a pair of shoes on her bare feet, and was glowing a "celestial rosy red." David stood where he was, and in half a minute Kirsty came in three leaps down the stair to him, to say that Francie was lying in the weem. In less than a minute the old soldier was out with the stable lantern, harnessing one of the horses, the oldest in the stable, good at standing, and not a bad walker. He called for no help, yet was round at the door so speedily as to astonish even Kirsty, who stood with her mother in the entrance by a pile of bedding. They put a mattress in the bottom of the cart, and plenty of blankets. Kirsty got in, lay down and covered herself up, to make the rough ambulance warm, and David drove off. They soon reached the weem and entered it.

The moment Kirsty had lighted the candle, David cried out, "Lassie, there's been a woman here!"

"It looks like it," answered Kirsty. "I was here myself, father!"

"Ay, ay! Of coorse, but here's clothes—woman's clothes! Where came they frae? Whose clothes can they be?"

"Whose but mine?" returned Kirsty, as she stepped to remove from his face the garment that covered his head.

"The Lord preserve us! To the verra stockin's upo' the hands o' 'im!"

"I had no dread, father, o' the Lord seein me as He made me!"

"My ain lassie!" murmured her father. "But, eh," he added, "we must hold oor tongues till we've done the thing we're sent to do!"

They bent at once to their task.

David was a strong man still, and Kirsty was as good at a lift as most men. They had no difficulty in raising Gordon between them, David taking his head and Kirsty his feet, but it was not without difficulty they got him through the passage. In the cart they covered him so that had he been a newborn baby, he could have taken no harm except it were by suffocation; then, with his head in Kirsty's lap, they drove home as fast as the old horse could step out.

In the meantime Marion had got her best room ready and warm. When they reached it, Francie was certainly still alive, and they made haste to lay him in the hot featherbed. In about an hour they thought he swallowed a little milk. Neither Kirsty nor her parents went to bed that night, and by one or other of them the patient was constantly attended.

Kirsty took the first watch, and was satisfied that his breathing grew more regular, and by and by stronger. After a while it became like that of one in a troubled sleep. He moved his head a little, and murmured like one dreaming painfully. She called her father, and told him he was saying words she could not understand. He took her place and sat near him, when presently his soldier ears, still sharp, heard indications of a hot siege. Once he started up on his elbow, and put his hand to the side of his head. For a moment he looked wildly awake, then sank back and went to sleep again.

As Marion was by him in the morning, all at once he spoke again, and more plainly.

"Go away, mother!" he said, "I am not mad. I am only troubled in my mind. I will tell my father you killed me."

Marion tried to rouse him, telling him his mother should not come near him. He did not seem to understand, but apparently her words soothed him, for he went to sleep once more.

He was gaunt and ghastly to look at. The scar on his face, which Kirsty had mistaken for the mark of her whip, but which was left by the splinter that woke him, remained red and disfiguring. But the worst of his look was in his eyes, whose glances wandered about uneasy and searching.

For a good many days he was like one awake yet dreaming, always dreading something, invariably starting when the door opened, and when quietest, gazing at the one by his bedside as if puzzled. In general he took what food they brought him, but at times refused it quite. They never left him alone for more than a moment.

So far were they from giving him up to his mother that the mere idea of letting her know he was with them never entered the mind of one of them. To the doctor they had called in, there was no need to explain the right by which they constituted themselves his guardians. Anyone would have judged it better for him to be with them than with her. David said to himself that when Francie wanted to leave them he should go, but he had sought refuge with them, and he should have it. Nothing should make him give him up except legal compulsion.

CHAPTER THIRTY-THREE

Francis Comes to Himself

One morning, as Kirsty sat beside him knitting, Francis started to his elbow as if to get up. Then he saw her, and lay down again with his eyes fixed upon her. She glanced at him now and then, but did not seem to notice him much. He gazed for two or three minutes, and then said, in a low, doubtful, almost timid voice, "Kirsty?"

"Ay, what is 't, Francie?" returned Kirsty, laying down her stocking.

"Is 't yerself, Kirsty?" he said.

"Ay, who ither, Francie!"

"Are ye angry at me, Kirsty?"

"No a grain. What makes ye ask sic a question?"

"Eh, but ye gave me sic a one wi' yer whip—jist here upo' the temple! Look."

He turned the side of this head toward her, and stroked the place, like a small, self-pitying child. Kirsty went to him, and kissed it like a mother. She had plainly perceived that such a scar could not be from her blow, but it added grievously to her pain that the poor head which she had struck had in the very same place been torn by a splinter—for so the doctor said. If her whip left any mark, the splinter had obliterated it.

"And," he resumed, "since ye called me a coward!"

"Did I do that, ill woman that I was!" she returned, with tenderest maternal soothing.

He reached his arms round her neck, drew her feebly toward him, laid his head on her shoulder and wept.

Kirsty put her arm round him, held him closer, and stroked his head with her other hand, murmuring words of much meaning though little sense. He drew back his head, looked at her beseechingly, and said, "Do ye think me a coward, Kirsty?"

"No wi' men," answered the truthful girl, who would not lie even in ministration to a mind diseased.

"Maybe ye think I ought to have struck ye back when ye struck me? I will be a coward then, let ye say what ye like. I never did, and I never will hit a lassie, let her kill me!"

"It wasna that, Francie. If I called ye a coward, it was that ye behaved so ill to Phemy."

"Eh, the bonny little Phemy! I had a'most forgotten her! How is she, Kirsty?"

"She's weel—verra weel," answered Kirsty. "She's dead."

"Dead!" echoed Gordon, with a cry, again raising himself on his elbow. "Surely it wasna—it wasna that the puir wee thing couldna forget me! The thing's no possible! I wasna worth it!"

"Na, na, it wasna one grain that! Her dyin had nothin to do wi' that, nor wi' you in any way. I dinna believe she was a hair worse for any nonsense ye said til her—shame o' ye as it was! She died upo' the Horn, one awful tempest o' a night. She couldna have suffered long, puir thing! She hadna the strength to suffer muckle. So away she went, and Steenie after her!" added Kirsty in a lower tone. But Francis did not seem to hear, and said no more for a little while.

"But I must tell ye the truth, Kirsty," he resumed. "There's them that says I'm a coward!"

"I heard one man say 't, only one, and him only once."

"And ye said til 'im, 'Ay, I have long kenned that!'"

"I told him whoever said it was a liar!"

"But ye believed it yerself, Kirsty!"

"Would ye have me a liar and hypocrite, to call fowk names for sayin what I believed myself?"

"But I am a coward, Kirsty!"

"Ye are not, Francie. I wouldna believe 't though yerself say 't! It's nothin but nonsense that's won in through the cracks ye got i' yer head, fightin. Ye was aye a daft kind o' creature, Francie! If anybody ever said it, make ye speed and get yer health again, and since ye can show him plain that he's a liar."

"But I tell ye, Kirsty, I ran away!"

"I fancy ye would have been nothing but a muckle idiot if ye hadna! Ye didna leave anybody in trouble, did ye noo?"

"No that I ken o'. Na, I didna do that. The fact was, but no blame to them, they all went away and left me my lone, sleepin. I must have been terrible tired."

"I telled ye so!" cried Kirsty. "Jist go over the story to me, Francie, and I shall tell ye whether ye're a coward or no. I dinna believe a bit o' 't! Ye never was, and never was likely to be a coward. I shall be at the bottom o' 't wi' whoever dare throw me sic a lie!"

But Francis showed such signs of excitement, as well as exhaustion, that Kirsty saw she must not let him talk longer.

"Or I'll tell ye what!" she added. "Ye'll tell father and mother and me the whole tale, this verra night, or maybe the morn's mornin. Ye must have an egg noo, and a drappy o' milk— creamy milk, Francie! Ye always liked that!" and she went to prepare the little meal.

In the evening, with the help of their questioning, he told them everything he could recall from the moment he woke to find the place abandoned, not omitting his terrors on the way, until he overtook the rear of the garrison.

"I dinna wonder ye was fleyt, Francie," said Kirsty, "I would have been fleyt myself, wantin my sword, and kennin no God to trust til! Ye must learn to ken Him, Francie, and then ye'll be feared at nothin!"

After that, his memory was only of utterly confused shapes, many of which must have been fancies. The only things he could report were the conviction pervading them all that he had disgraced himself, and the consciousness that everyone treated him as a deserter, and gave him the cold shoulder.

His next recollection was of coming home to, or rather finding himself with his mother who, the moment she saw him, flew into a rage, struck him in the face, and called him coward. She must have taken him, he thought, to some place where there were people about him who would not let him alone, but he could remember nothing more until he found himself creeping into a hole which he seemed to know, thinking he was a fox with the hounds after him.

"What's my clothes like, Kirsty?" he asked at this point.

"They were no that grand," answered Kirsty, her eyes smarting with the coming tears, "but ye'll ne'er see a stitch o' them again. I put them away."

"Why'll I wind up no wantin them?" he rejoined, with a tremor of anxiety in his voice.

"We'll see aboot that, time enough," answered Kirsty.

"But my mither may be after me! I would fain be up! There's no sayin what she mightna be up til! She canna bide me!"

"Dread ye nothin, Francie. Ye're no a match for my leddy, but I shall be atween ye and her. She's no so fearsome as she thinks!"

"I left some guid enough clothes there when I went away, and I daresay they're i' my room yet, if only I kenned hoo to get them!"

"I shall go and get them til ye—the verra day ye're fit to rise. But ye mustna speak a word more the night."

CHAPTER THIRTY-FOUR

Kirsty Bestirs Herself

They held a long consultation that night as to what they must do. Plainly the first and most important thing was to rid Francis of the delusion that he had disgraced himself in the eyes of his fellow officers. This would at once wake him as from a bad dream to the reality of his condition. Convinced of the unreality of the idea that possessed him, he would at once, they believed, resume his place in the march of his generation through life. They set their wits to work to find a way to expose the truth, and it was almost at once clear to David that the readiest way would be to contact any they could reach of the officers under whom he had served. But by this time his regiment had, with the rest of the Company's soldiers, passed into the service of the Queen. Francis, even if he were fit to be questioned, could give no information regarding their specific whereabouts; so David resolved to apply to Sir Haco Macintosh, Archibald Gordon's successor in the command, for assistance in finding those who could bear the testimony he desired to possess.

"Don't ye think, father," said Kirsty, "it would be the surest and speediest way for me to go myself to Sir Haco?"

"It would be that, Kirsty!" answered David. "There's nothin like the bodily presence o' the livin soul to make things go!"

Although at first Marion was appalled at the thought of Kirsty alone in such a huge city as Edinburgh, she could not help assenting. The next morning Kirsty started, bearing a letter from her father to his old officer, in which he begged for her the favor of a few minutes' conference on business concerning her father and the son of the late Colonel Gordon.

Sir Haco had retired from the service some years before the mutiny, and was living in one of the serenely gloomy squares of the Scots capital. Kirsty left her letter at the door. When she called the next day, she was shown to the library, where Lady Macintosh as well as Sir Haco awaited, with curious and kindly interest, the daughter of the man they had known so well, and respected so much.

When Kirsty entered the room, dressed very simply in a gown of dark cloth and a plain straw bonnet, the impression she at once made was more than favorable, and they received her with a kindness and courtesy that made her feel welcome. They were indeed of her own kind.

Sir Haco was one of the few men who, regarding constantly the reality and not the show of things, keep throughout their life a great part of their youth and all their childhood. Deeper far in his heart than any of the honors he had received, all unsought but none undeserved, lay the memory of a happy and reverential boyhood. Sprung from a peasant stock, his father was a man of "high erected thought seated in a heart of courtesy."

He was well matched with his wife who, though born to a far higher social position in which simplicity is rarer, was, like him, true and humble and strong. They had one daughter, who grew up only to die. The moment they saw Kirsty, their hearts went out to her.

For there was in Kirsty that unassumed, unconscious dignity, that simple propriety, that naturalness of a carriage neither trammeled nor warped by thought of self, which at once awakes confidence and regard. Her sweet, unaffected "book English," in which appeared no attempt at speaking like a fine lady, no disastrous endeavor to avoid her country's utterance, revealed at once her genuine cultivation. Sir Haco said afterward that when she spoke Scots it was good and thorough, and when she spoke

English it was Wordsworthian.

Listening to her first words, and reminded of the solemn sententious way in which Sergeant Barclay used to express himself, his face rose clear in his mind's eye, he saw it as it were reflected in his daughter's, and broke out with, "Eh, lassie, but ye're like yer father! Sit ye doon, and tell us all aboot him!"

Kirsty did as she was told. She began at the beginning, and explained first, what doubtless Sir Haco knew at least something of before, the relation between her father and Colonel Gordon, and why their family had always felt it their business to look after the young laird. Then she told how, after a long interval, during which they could do nothing, a sad opportunity had at length been given them of at least attempting to serve him, and it was for aid in the attempt that she now sought Sir Haco, who could direct her toward the procuring of certain information.

"And what sort of information do you think I can give or get for you, Miss Barclay?" asked Sir Haco.

"I'll explain the thing to ye, sir, in as few words as I can," answered Kirsty, dropping her English. "The yoong laird has taken 't intil his head that he didna carry himself like a man i' the siege, and it's grown to be in him what they call a fixed idea. He was left, ye see, sir, all alone i' the beleaguered town, and I fancy the sudden wakin and the discovery that he was there his lone, jist put him beside himself."

She told the whole story, as they had gathered it from Francis, mingling it with some elucidatory suggestions of her own.

"Ye see, sir, and my leddy," Kirsty explained in conclusion, "he was little better nor a laddie, and fowk that sore needs company, like Francie, misses company over sore. Some men's no able, my leddy, to take counsel wi' their own hearts, as women learn to do. And so, when he came oot o' the fright, he was over sore upon himself for bein i' the fright. For it seems to me there's no shame in bein frighted, so long as ye dinna serve and obey the fright, but trust in Him that sees, and do what ye have to do. Nobody than kenned Francie as I did could ever believe he had more fear in 'is heart nor was lawfu' and reasonable, so long as he was in his right mind. Beyond that none but his Maker can judge him. The laddie—the man, I should say— he's no to be persuaded oot o' the fancy o' his own cowardice, and I dinna believe he'll ever win oot o' 't wantin the testimony o' his fellow officers, who o' thcm may be left to grant the same. And I canna but think that for his father's sake, it would be gracious to take him intil the Queen's service, and let him hold on fightin for 'is country, wherever it may please Her Majesty to want him. Oot where he was afore might be best for him—I dinna ken. It would be to put his country's seal upo' their word."

"Surely, Miss Barclay, you wouldn't set the poor lad in the forefront of danger again!" said Lady Macintosh.

"I would that, my leddy! I canna but think the army, savin for this misadventure—if there be any sic thing as misadventure— had a fair chance o' makin a man o' Francie. I canna help doobtin if anythin less'll ever restore him til himself but restorin him til 'is former position. It would give him the best chance o' showin til himself that there wasna a hair o' the coward upon him."

"But," said Sir Haco, "would Her Majesty be justified in taking the risk involved? Would it not be to peril many for a doubtful good to one?"

Kirsty was silent, with downcast eyes.

"For my part," said Lady Macintosh, "I can't help thinking that the love of a good woman like yourself must do more for the poor fellow than the approval of all the soldiers in the world. Pardon me, Haco."

"Indeed, my lady, you're perfectly right!" returned her husband with a smile.

But Lady Macintosh hardly heard him, so startled, almost so frightened was she at the indignation instantly on Kirsty's countenance.

"Putna things intil any head, my leddy, that the heart would never put there. It would be an ill fulfillin o' my father's duty til his auld colonel, no to say his auld friend, to consider sic a notion!"

"I beg your pardon, Miss Barclay. I was wrong to venture the remark. But may I say in excuse, that it is not unnatural to imagine a young woman, doing so much for a young man, just a little bit in love with him?"

"I would fain have yer leddyship un'erstand," returned Kirsty, "that my father, my mother, and myself, we're jist one and no more. No one o' us has a wish that doesna belong to all three. It's aye been my one ambition to help my father and mother to do what they wanted. I never desired marriage, my leddy, and if I did, it wouldna be wi' sic as Francie Gordon, weel as I love him, for we were bairnies, and laddie and lassie thegither. I wouldna have a man it was for me to find fault wi'!"

Not to believe the honest glow in Kirsty's face, and the clear confident assertion of her eyes, would have shown a poor creature in whom the faculty of belief was undeveloped.

Sir Haco and Lady Macintosh insisted on Kirsty's taking her abode with them while she was in Edinburgh, and Kirsty, her heart drawn to her new friends, gladly consented. Before a week was over, like understanding like, her hostess felt as if Kirsty were a daughter until now long waiting for her somewhere in the infinite.

That same morning, Sir Haco sat down at his desk, and began writing to every officer alive who had served with Francis Gordon, requesting to know his feeling, and that of the regiment about him. Within three days he received the first of the answers. They all described Gordon as rather a scatterbrain, as not the less a favorite with officers and men, and as always showing the courage of a man, or rather of a boy, seeing he not unfrequently acted with a reprehensible recklessness that smacked a little of display.

"That's Francie himself!" cried Kirsty, with tears in her eyes, when her host read to her the first result of his inquiry.

Within a fortnight he received also, from one high in office, the assurance that, if Mr. Gordon, on his recovery wished to enter Her Majesty's service, he should have his commission.

While her husband was thus kindly occupied, Lady Macintosh was showing Kirsty every loving attention she could think of, and, in taking her about Edinburgh and its neighborhood, found that the country girl knew far more of the history of

Scotland than she did herself.

She would gladly have made her acquainted with some of her friends, but Kirsty shrank from the proposal. She could not forget how her hostess had herself misinterpreted the interest she took in Francis Gordon. As soon as she felt that she could do so without seeming ungrateful, she bade her friends farewell, and hastened home, carrying with her copies of the answers which Sir Haco had up to that time received.

When she arrived it was with such a glad heart that, at sight of Francis in her father's Sunday clothes, she laughed so merrily that her mother said, "The lassie must be doomed!" Haggard as Francis looked, the old twinkle awoke in his eye reponsive to her joyous amusement, and David, coming in the next moment from putting up the gray mare with which he had met the coach to bring Kirsty home, saw the three of them laughing in such an abandonment of mirth as, though unaware of the immediate motive, he could not help joining.

The same evening Kirsty went to the castle, and Mrs. Bremner needed no persuasion to find the suit which the young laird had left in his room, and gave it to her to carry to its owner. When he woke the next morning, Francis saw the gray garments lying by his bedside in place of David's black, and felt the better for the sight.

The letters Kirsty had brought, working along with returning health, and the surrounding love and sympathy most potent of all, speedily dispelled his yet lingering delusion. It had occasionally returned in force while Kirsty was away, but now it left him altogether.

CHAPTER THIRTY-FIVE

A Great Gulf

By midsummer Francis Gordon was well, though thin and looking rather delicate. Kirsty and he had walked together to the top of the Horn, and there sat in the heart of old memories. The sun was clouded above; the boggy basin lay dark below, with its rim of heathery hills not yet in bloom, and its bottom of peaty marsh, green and black, with here and there a shining spot. The growing crops of the far-off farms on the other side but little affected the general impression the view gave of a waste world; yet the wide expanse of heaven and earth lifted the heart of Kirsty with an indescribable sense of presence, purpose, promise. For was this not the country on which, fresh from God, she first opened the eyes of her life? It was the visible region in which all her efforts had gone forth, in which all the food of her growth had been gathered, in which all her joys had come to her, in which all her loves had had their scope, the place from where by and by she would go away to find her brother with the Bonny Man!

Francis saw without heeding. His heart was not uplifted. His earthly future, a future of his own imagining, drew him.

"This willna do any longer, Kirsty!" he said at length. "I mustna be idle 'cause I'm happy once more—thanks to you! Little did I think ever to raise my head again! But noo I must be at my work! I'm fit enough!"

"I'm right glad to hear 't!" answered Kirsty. "I was jist thinkin long for word o' the sort frae ye, Francie. I didna want to be the first to speak o' 't."

"And I was just thinkin long to hear ye speak o' 't!" returned Francis. "I wanted to do 't as the thing ye would have o' me!"

"Even then, Francie, ye wouldna have been doin 't to please me, and that pleases me weel! I would be none pleased to think ye doin 't for me! It would give me a sore heart, Francie!"

"What for that, Kirsty?"

" 'Cause it would show ye no a man yet! A man's a man that does what is right, what's pleasin to the verra heart o' right. Ye'll please me best by no wantin to please me, and ye'll please God best by doin what He's put intil yer heart as the right thing—the bonny and true thing, though ye should die i' the doin o' 't. Tell me what ye're thinkin o' doin."

"What but goin after this new commission they have promised me? There's always a guid chance o' fightin upo' the borders—the frontiers, as they call them!"

Kirsty sat silent. She had been thinking much of what Francis ought to do, and had changed her mind on the point since the time when she talked to Sir Haco.

"Isna that what ye would have me do, Kirsty?" he said, when he found she continued silent. "A body's no a gowk for wantin guid advice!"

"No, that's true enough! What for would ye want to go fightin?"

"To show the warld I'm none o' what my mither called me."

"And shown that, hoo muckle the better man would ye be for 't? Mind ye it's one thing to be, and anither to show. *Be* ye must; *show* ye needna."

"I dinna ken. I might be growin better all the time!"

"And ye might be growin worse. What the better would any neighbor be for ye goin fightin? Wouldna it be all for yerself? Is there nothin given intil yer hand to do—nothin nearer hame nor that? Surely o' twa things, one near and one far, the near comes first!"

"I dinna ken. I thought ye wanted me to go!"

"Ay, rather nor bide at hame doin nothin, but mightna there be something better to do?"

"I dinna ken. I thought to please ye, Kirsty, but it seems nothin will!"

"Ay, that's where the mischief lies. Ye thought to please *me!*"

"I did think to please you, Kirsty! I thought, once done weel afore the warld as my father did, I might have the face to come hame to you, and say—'Kirsty, will ye have me?' "

"Aye the same auld Francie!" said Kirsty with a deep sigh. "Weel?"

"I tell ye, Francie, i' the name o' God, I'll never have ye on no sic terms! Suppose I was to marry somebody when ye was away provin to yerself, and all the rest that never misdoobted ye, that ye was a brave man—what would ye do when ye came hame?"

"Nothin o' mortal guid! Take to the drink, maybe."

"Ye tell me that, and ye think, wi' my eyes open to ken that ye say true, I would marry ye? A man like you! Eh, Francie, Francie! Ye're no worth my takin, and ye're no likely to be worth the takin o' any honest woman! Can ye possibly imagine a woman marryin a man that she kenned would go to drink? Ye make my heart sore, Francie! I have done my best wi' ye, all for nothin!"

"For the life o' me, Kirsty, what are ye drivin at? I canna but think ye're usin me as ye wouldna like to be used yerself!"

" 'Deed I would not like it if I was o' your breed, Francie! Man, did ye never once i' yer life think what ye *had* to do—what was given ye to do—what it was yer *duty* to do?"

"No so often, dooblless, as I ought. But I'm ready to hear ye tell me my duty. I'm no past reasonin wi'!"

"Did ye never hear that ye're to love yer neighbor as yerself?"

"I'm doin that wi' all my heart, Kirsty, and that ye ken as weel as I do myself!"

"Ye mean me, Francie! And ye call that lovin me, to have me marry a man that's no man at all! But it's no me that's yer neighbor, Francie!"

"Who *is* my neighbor, Kirsty?"

"Yer neighbor's jist whoever lies next to ye i' need o' yer help. If ye read the tale o' the guid Samaritan wi' any sort o' gumption, that's what ye'll read intil 't and nought else. The man or woman ye can help, ye have to be neighbor til."

"I want to help you."

"Ye canna help me. I'm in no need o' yer help. And the question's no where's the man I *might* help, but where's the man I *must* help."

"Kirsty, i' the name o' God, who *is* my neighbor?"

"Yer own mither."

"My mither! *Her* oot o' all the warld? I never came upo' spark o' reason intil her!"

"Mightna she be that one, oot o' all the warld, ye never showed spark o' reason til?"

"There's no place in her for reason to go til!"

"Ye never tried her wi' 't! Ye would argue wi' her more nor plenty, but did ye ever show her reason i' yer behavior?"

"Weel, ye *are* turnin against me—you that saved my life frae her! Didna I tell you hoo, when I went home at last and went to her, for she was always guid to me when I wasna weel, she fell oot upo' me like a verra deevil, ragin and callin me ill names, that I jist ran frae the hoose—and ye ken where ye found me! If it hadna been for you, I would have been dead. I was worse nor dead already! What way *can* I be neighbor to *her*? It would be nothing but cat and dog atween us frae mornin to night!"

"One body canna be cat and dog both! And the dog's as ill's the cat!"

"Any dog would yowl if ye threw a kettle o' boilin water over him!"

"Did she tell that til ye?"

"She hinted at it. I ran frae her. She had the toddy kettle in her hand, and she splashed it in her own face tryin to fling 't at me."

"Maybe she didna ken ye!"

"She kenned me weel enough. She called me by my own as weel as ither names."

"Ye're jist croonin my argument, Francie! Yer mither's jist

perishin o' drink! She drinks and drinks and, by what I hear, cares for nought else. She hasna the brains noo, if ever she had them, to guide herself. Is Satan to grip her 'cause ye willna be neighbor til her and hold him off o' her? I ken ye're a guid son so far as let her do as she likes and take almost all the siller, but that's what greases the axle o' the cart the deevil's gotten her intil! I ken weel she hasna been muckle o' a mither til ye, but ye're her son when all's said. And there can be nothing ye're called upon to do, so long as she's i' the grip o' the enemy, but drag her oot o' 't. If ye dinna that, ye'll never be oot o' his grip yersel. Ye come oot thegither, or ye bide thegither."

Francis sat speechless. "It's impossible!" he said at length.

"Francie," rejoined Kirsty, very quietly and solemnly, "ye're yer mither's keeper, her next neighbor. Are ye goin to do yer duty by her, or are ye not?"

"I canna—I darena! I'm a coward afore her."

"If ye let her go on to disgrace yer father, no to say yersel—and that by means o' what's yours and no hers, I'll say myself that ye're a coward."

"Come hame wi' me and take my part, and I'll promise ye to do my best."

"Ye must take yer own part, and ye must take her part too against herself."

"It's no to be thought o', Kirsty!"

"Ye willna?"

"I canna alone. I willna try 't. It would be worse nor useless."

Kirsty rose, turning her face homeward. Francis sprang to his feet. She was already three yards from him.

"Kirsty! Kirsty!" he cried, going after her.

She went straight for home, never showing by turn of head, by hesitation of step, or by change of carriage, that she heard his voice or his feet behind her.

When they had thus gone two or three hundred yards, he quickened his pace, and laid his hand on her arm.

She stopped and faced him. He dropped his hand, grew yet whiter, and said not a word. She walked on again. Like one in a dream, he followed, his head hanging, his eyes on the heather.

She went faster. He was falling behind her, but did not know it. Down and down the hill he followed, and only at the earth house lifted his head: she was nearly over the opposite brae! He had let her go! He might yet have overtaken her, but he knew that he had lost her.

He had no home, no refuge! Then first, not when alone in the beleaguered city, he knew desolation. He had never knocked at the door of heaven, and earth had closed hers! An angel who needed no flaming sword to make her awful, held the gate of his lost paradise against him. None but she could open to him, and he knew that, like God himself, Kirsty was inexorable. Left alone with that last terrible look from the eyes of the one being he loved, he threw himself in despair on the ground. True love is an awful thing, not to the untrue only, but sometimes to the growing-true, for to everything that can be burned it is a consuming fire. Never more, it seemed, would those eyes look in at his soul's window without that sad, indignant repudiation in them! He rose, and crept into the earthhouse.

Kirsty lost herself in prayer as she went. "Lord, I have done all I can!" she said. "Until Thou hast done somethin by Thyself, I can no nothin more. He's i' Thy hands still, I praise Thee, though he's oot o' mine! Lord, if I have done him any ill, forgive me, a puir human body canna ken always the best! Dinna let him suffer for my ignorance, whether I be to blame for 't or no. I will try to do whatever Thou makest plain to me."

By the time she reached home she was calm. Her mother saw and respected her solemn mood, gave her a mother's look, and said nothing. She knew that Kirsty, lost in her own thoughts, was in good company.

In the soul of Francis Gordon was passing the most mysterious of all vital movements, a regeneration, a transition, was there—how initiated, God only knows. Francis knew neither whence it came nor whither it went. He was being reborn from above. The change was in himself, the birth was that of his will. It was his own highest action, therefore all God's. He was passing from death into life, and knew it no more than the babe knows that he is being born. The change was into a new state of being, the very existence of which most men are incredulous, for it is beyond preconception, capable only of being experienced. Thorough as is the change, the man knows himself the same man, and yet would rather cease to be, than return to what he was.

Francis knew nothing of all this. He only felt he must knock on the door behind which Kirsty lived. Kirsty could not open the door to him, but there was One who could, and Francis could knock! "God help me!" he cried, as he lay on his face to live, where one he had lain on his face to die. The sepulchre is for the rising again. The world itself is one vast sepulchre for the heavenly resurrection. We are all busy within the walls of our tomb burying our dead, that the corruptible may perish, and the incorruptible go free. Francis Gordon came out of that earth house a risen man: his will was born. He climbed again to the spot where Kirsty and he had sat together, and there, with the vast clear heaven over his head, threw himself once more on his face, and lifted up his heart to the Heart whence he came.

CHAPTER THIRTY-SIX

The Neighbors

He had eaten nothing since the morning, and felt like one in a calm ethereal dream as he walked home to Weelset in the soft dusk of an evening that would never be night, but die into the day. No one saw him enter the house, no one met him on the ancient spiral stair as, with apprehensive anticipation, he sought the drawing room.

He had just set his foot on the little landing by its door when a wild scream came from the room. He flung the door open and darted in. His mother rushed into his arms, enveloped from foot to head in a cone of fire. She was making, in wild flight, for the stair, to reach which would have been death to her. Francis held her fast, but she struggled so wildly that he had actually to throw her on the floor ere he could do anything to deliver her. Then he flung on her the rug, the tablecloth, his coat, and one of the curtains, tearing it fiercely from the rings. Having got all these close around her, he rang the bell, but had to ring three times, for service in that house was deadened by frequent fury of summons. Two of the maids—there was no manservant in the house now—laid their mistress on a mattress, and carried her to her room. Gordon's hands and arms were so severely burned that he could do nothing beyond directing. He thought he had never felt pain before.

The doctor was sent for, and came speedily. Having examined them, he said Mrs. Gordon's injuries would have caused him no anxiety but for her habits. Their consequences might be very serious, and every possible care must be taken of her.

Disabled as he was, Francis sat by her till the morning, and the night's nursing did far more for himself than for his mother. For as he saw how she suffered, and interpreted her moans by what he had felt and was still feeling in his own hands and arms, a great pity awoke in him. What a lost life his mother's had been! Was this to be the end of it? The old kindness she had shown him in his childhood and youth, especially when he was in any bodily trouble, came back upon him, and a new love, gathering up in it all the intermittent love of days long gone by, sprang to life in his heart, and he saw that the one thing given him to do was to deliver his mother.

As long as she was incapable of resisting, annoying, or deceiving him, the task seemed, if not easy, yet not irksome. But the time quickly came when he realized that the continuous battle, rather than war of duty and inclination, must be fought and in some measure won in himself before he could hope to stir up any smallest skirmish of sacred warfare in the soul of his mother.

What added to the acerbities of this preliminary war was that the very nature of the contest required actions which showed not only unbecoming a son, but mean and disgraceful in themselves. There was no pride, pomp, or circumstance of glorious war in this poor, domestic strife, this seemingly sordid and unheroic, miserably unheroic, yet high, eternal contest! But now that Francis was awake to his duty, the best of his nature awoke to meet its calls, and he drew upon a growing store of love for strength to thwart the desires of her he loved. Francis learned not to mind looking penurious and tyrannical, selfish, heartless, and unsympathetic, in the endeavor to be truly loving and lovingly true.

He had not Kirsty to support him, but he could now go higher than to Kirsty for the help he needed. He went to the same fountain from which Kirsty herself drew her strength. At the same time frequent thought of her filled him with glad assurance of her sympathy, which was in itself a wondrous aid. He neither saw nor sought to see her. He would not go near her before at least she already knew from other sources what would give her the hope that he was trying to do right.

The gradually approaching strife between mother and son burst out the same moment in which the devilish thirst awoke to its cruel tyranny. It was a mercy to both of them that it reasserted itself while yet the mother was helpless toward any indulgence of her passion. Francis was no longer afraid of her, but it was easier because of her condition, although not the less painful for him to frustrate her desire. Neither did it make it the less painful that already her countenance, which the outward fire had not half so much disfigured as that which she had herself applied inwardly, had begun to remind him of the face he had long ago loved a little. This only made him, if possible, yet more determined that not one shilling of his father's money should go to the degradation of his mother. That she lusted and desired to have was the worst of reasons why she should obtain! A compelled temperance was in itself, of course, worthless; but that alone could give opportunity for the waking of what soul was left her. Puny as it was, that might then begin to grow; it might become aware of the bondage to which it had been subjected, and begin to long for liberty.

In carrying out his resolution, Francis found it specially hard to fight the good in himself. The lower forms of love rose against the higher and had to be put down. To see the scintillation of his mother's eyes at the sound of any liquid, and know how easily he could give her an hour of false happiness, tore his heart, while her fierce abuse hardly passed the portals of his brain. Her condition was so pitiful that her words could not make him angry. She would declare it was he who set her clothes on fire, and as soon as she was up again, she would publish to the world what a coward and sneak he showed himself from morning to night. Had Francis been what he once was, his mother and he must soon have come as near absolute hatred as is possible to the human; but he was now so different that the worst answer he ever gave her was, "Mother, you *know* you don't mean it!"

"I mean it with all my heart and soul, Francis," she replied, glaring at him.

He stooped to kiss her on the forehead. She struck him on the face so that the blood sprang. He went back a step, and stood looking at her sadly as he wiped it away.

"Crying!" she said. "You always were a coward, Francis!"

But the word had no more any sting for him.

"I'm alright mother. My nose got in the way!" he answered, restoring his handkerchief to his pocket.

"It's the doctor puts him up to it!" said Mrs. Gordon to herself. "But we shall soon be rid of him now! If there's any more of this nonsense then, I shall have to shut Francis up again! That will teach him how to behave to his mother!"

When at length Mrs. Gordon was able to go about the house again, it was at once to discover that things were not to be as they had been. Then deepened the combat. The battle of the warrior is with confused noises and garments rolled in blood, but how much harder and worthier battles are fought, not in shining armor, but amid filth and squalor physical as well as moral, on a field of wretched and wearisome commonplace!

It was essential to success that there should be no traitor among the servants, and Francis had made them understand what his measures were. One day, she was found under the influence of strong drink. He summoned all the servants and told them that, sooner than fail of his end, he would part with the whole household, and should be driven to it if no one revealed how the thing had come to pass. Thereupon the youngest, a mere girl, burst into tears, and confessed that she had procured the whiskey. Hardly thinking it possible his mother should have money in her possession, so careful was he to prevent it, he questioned, and found that she had herself provided the half-crown required, and that her mistress had given her in return a valuable brooch, an heirloom, which was hers only to wear, not to give. He took this from her, repaid her the half-crown, gave her her wages up to the next term, and sent her home immediately. Her father being one of his own tenants, he rode to his place the next morning, laid before him the whole matter, and advised him to keep the girl at home for a year or two.

This one success gave such a stimulus to Mrs. Gordon's passion that her rage with her keeper, which had been abating a little, blazed up at once as fierce as at first. But miserable as the whole thing was, Gordon held out bravely. At the end of six months, however, during which no fresh indulgence had been possible to her, he had not gained the least ground for hoping that any poorest growth of strength, or even any waking desire toward betterment, had taken place in her.

All this time he had not once been to Corbyknowe. But Francis had been seeing David Barclay three or four times a week. He had told David how he stood with Kirsty, and how, while refusing him, she had shown him his duty to his mother. He told him also that he now saw things with other eyes, and was endeavoring to do what was right. But he dared not speak to her on the subject lest she should think after what had passed between them that he was doing for her sake what ought to be done for its own. He said to David that as he was no man of business, and must give his best attention to his mother, he found it impossible for the present to acquaint himself with the state of the property, or indeed attend to it in any serviceable manner; and he begged him, as his father's friend and his own, to look into his affairs and, so far as his other duties would permit, place things on at least a better footing.

To this petition, David had at once gladly consented.

He found everything connected with the property in a sad condition. The agent, although honest, was weak, and had so given way to Mrs. Gordon that much havoc had been made, and much money wasted. He was now in bad health, and had lost all heart for his work. But he had turned nothing to his own advantage, and was quite ready, under David's supervision, to do his best for the restoration of order and the curtailment of expenses.

All that David now saw in his association with the young laird convinced him that he was at length a man of conscience, cherishing steady purposes. He reported at home what he saw, and said what he believed, and his wife and daughter perceived plainly that his heart was lighter than it had been for many a day. Kirsty listened, said little, asked a question here and there, and thanked God. For her father brought her not only the good news that Francis was doing his best for his mother, but that he had begun to open his eyes to the fact that he had his part in the well-being of all on his land, that the property was not his for the filling of his pockets, or for the carrying out of schemes of his own, but for the general and individual comfort and progress.

Mrs. Gordon's temper seemed for a time to have changed from fierce to sullen, but by degrees she began to show herself not altogether indifferent to the continuous attentions of her inexorable son. It is true she received them as her right, but he yielded her a right immeasurably beyond that she would have claimed. He would play checkers or cribbage with her for hours at a time, and every day for months read Scott and Dickens to her as long as she would listen.

One day, when after much entreaty, she consented to go out for a drive with him, round to the door came a beautiful new carriage, and such a pair of horses as she could not help expressing satisfaction with. Francis told her they were at her command; but if ever she took unfair advantage of them, he would send both carriage and horses away.

She was furious at his daring to speak so to *her*, and had almost returned to her room, but thought better of it and went with him. She did not, however, speak a word to him the whole way. The next morning he let her go alone. After that, he sometimes went with her, and sometimes not. The desire of his heart was to behold her a free woman.

She was quite steady for a while, and her spirits began to return. The hopes of her son rose high; he almost ceased to fear.

CHAPTER THIRTY-SEVEN

Kirsty Gives Advice

It was again midsummer, and just a year since they parted on the Horn, when Francis appeared at Corbyknowe, and found Kirsty in the kitchen. She received him as if nothing had ever come between them; but at once noting he was in trouble, proposed they should go out together. It was a long way to be silent, but they had reached the spot, where they once had raced each other, before either of them said a word.

"Will ye no sit, Kirsty?" said Francis at length.

For answer she dropped on the same stone where she was sitting when she challenged him to it, and Francis took his seat on its neighbor.

"I have had a sore time o' 't since I showed ye plain hoo little I was worth yer notice, Kirsty!" he began.

"Ay," returned Kirsty, "but every hour o' 't has shown what the real Francis was!"

"I kenna, Kirsty. All I can say is that I doona think so muckle o' myself as I did then."

"And I think a heap more o' ye," answered Kirsty. "I canna but think ye upo' the right road noo, Francie!"

"I hope I am, but I'm always findin oot something that'll never do."

"And ye'll keep findin' oot that so long as there's anythin left

199

but what's like Himself."

"I understand ye, Kirsty. But I came to ye the day, no to say anythin aboot myself, but jist 'cause I couldna do wantin yer help. I wouldna have presumed but that I thought, although I dinna deserve 't, for auld kindness ye would say what ye would advise."

"I'll do that, Francie—no for auld kindness, but for kindness never auld. What's wrong wi' ye?"

"Kirsty, woman, she's broken oot again!"

"I dinna wonder. I have heard o' sic things."

"It's jist taken the pith oot o' me! What *am* I to do?"

"Ye canna do better nor weel. Jist begin again."

"I had bought her a bonny carriage, wi' as fine a pair as ever ye saw, Kirsty, as I daresay yer father has telled ye. And they warna lost upon her, for she had aye a guid eye for a horse, and up til yesterday, all was weel, till I was thinkin I could trust her. But i' the afternoon, as she was oot for an airin, one o' the horses dropped a shoe, and thinkin nothin o' the risk til a human soul, but only o' the risk til the puir horse, the fool fellow stopped at a smithy no farther nor the next door frae a public, and took the horse intil the smith, leavin the smith's lad at the head o' the ither horse. So what should my leddy do but oot upo' the side *frae* the smithy, and away round the back o' the carriage to the public, and in! Whether she took anythin there I dinna ken, but she must have brought a bottle hame wi' her, for this mornin she was tipsy as e'er ye saw man in market!"

He broke down, and wept like a child.

"And what did ye do?" asked Kirsty.

"I said nothin. I jist went to the coachman and made him put his horses to, and take his dinner wi' him, and drive straight away til Aberdeen, and leave the carriage where I bought it, and do siclike wi' the horses and come hame by the coach."

As he ended the sad tale, he glanced up at Kirsty, and saw her regarding him with a look such as he had never seen, imagined, or dreamed of before. It lasted but a moment. Her eyes dropped, and she went on with the knitting which, as in the old days, she had brought with her.

"Noo, Kirsty, what am I to do next?" he said.

"Have ye nothin i' yer own mind?" she asked.

"Nothin."

"Weel, we'll away home!" she returned, rising. "Maybe, as we go, we'll get light!"

They walked in silence. Now and then Francis would look at Kirsty's face, to see if anything was coming, but saw only that she was sunk in thought. He would not hurry her, and said not a word. He knew she would speak the moment she had what she thought worth saying.

Kirsty, recalling what her father had repeatedly said of Mrs. Gordon's management of a horse in her young days, had fallen to wondering how one who so well understood the equine nature, could be so incapable of understanding the human; for certainly she had little known either Archibald Gordon or David Barclay, and quite as little her own son. Having come to the conclusion that the incapacity was caused by overpowering affection for the one human creature she ought not to love, Kirsty found her thoughts return to the sole faculty her father yielded Mrs. Gordon—that of riding a horse as he ought to be ridden. She then remembered a conclusion she had lately read somewhere, that a man ought to regard his neighbor as specially characterized by this or that virtue or capacity, whatever it might be, that distinguished him. *That* was as the doorplate indicating the proper entrance to his inner house. A moment more and Kirsty thought she saw a way in which Francis might gain a firmer hold on his mother, as well as provide her with a pleasure that might work toward her redemption.

"Francie," she said, "I have thought o' somethin. My father has aye said that yer mother as a guid rider in her young days, and this is what I would have ye do. Go straight away, wherever ye think best, and buy for her the best-lookin, best-tempered, handiest, and easiest goin leddy's horse ye can lay yer hand upo', and ye must jist ride wi' her wherever she goes."

"I'll do 't, Kirsty. I canna go straight away, though. I fear she has whiskey left, and there's no sayin what she might do afore I got back. I must go hame first."

"I'm no clear upo' that. Ye canna go and search all the hoose she calls her ain! That would anger her terrible. Nor can ye lay hands upon her, and take frae her by force. A woman might do that, but a man, and specially a woman's own one son, canna weel do 't—that is, if there's any ither course that can be followed. It seems to me ye must take the risk o' her bottle. And it may be no ill thing that she should disgrace herself oot and oot. Anyway wi' bein away, and comin back wi' the horse i' yer hand ye'll come afore her like bringin wi' ye a fresh beginnin, a new order o' things like, and that way avoid words wi' her."

Francis remained in thoughtful silence.

"I have little fear," pursued Kirsty, "but we'll get her frae the drink althegither, and the hope is we may get something better put intil her. Bein tipsy whiles isna the main difficulty. But I beg yer pardon, Francie! I mustna forget that she's yer mither!"

"If ye would but take her and me thegither, Kirsty, it would be a grand thing for both o' us! Wi' you to take the half o' 't, I might stand up under the weight o' my responsibility!"

"I'm takin my share o' that, anyway, darin to advise ye, Francie! Noo go, laddie. Go straight away and buy the horse."

CHAPTER THIRTY-EIGHT

Mrs. Gordon

When Mrs. Gordon came to herself, she thought to behave as if nothing had happened, and rang the bell to order her carriage. The maid informed her that the coachman had driven away with it before lunch, and had not said where he was going.

"Driven away with it!" cried her mistress, starting to her feet. "I gave him no orders!"

"I saw the laird givin him directions, mem," rejoined the maid.

Mrs. Gordon sat down again. She began to remember what her son had said when first he gave her the carriage.

"Where did he send him?" she asked.

"I dinna ken, mem."

"Go and ask the laird to step this way."

"Please, mem, he's no i' the hoose. I saw him go oot hours ago."

"Did he go in the carriage? Perhaps he's come home by this time!"

"I'm sure he's no that, mem."

Mrs. Gordon went to her room, all but finished the bottle of whiskey, and threw herself upon her bed.

Toward morning she woke with aching head and miserable mind. Now dozing, now tossing about in wretchedness, she lay till the afternoon. No one came near her, and she wanted no one.

At length, dizzy and despairing, her head in torture, and her heart sick, she managed to get out of bed, and, unable to walk, literally crawled to the cupboard in which she had put away the precious bottle. Joy! There was yet a glass in it! With the mouth of it to her lips, she was tilting it up to drain the last drop, when the voice of her son came cheerily from the drive, on which her window looked down.

"Mother, come see what I've brought you!" he called.

Fear came upon her. She took the bottle from her mouth, put it again in the cupboard, and crept back to her bed, her brain like a hive buzzing with devils.

When Francis entered the house, he was not surprised to learn that she had not left her room. He did not try to see her.

The next morning she felt a little better, and had some tea. Still she did not care to get up. She shrank from meeting her son, and the more able she grew to think, the more unwilling she was to see him. He came to her room, but she heard him coming, turned her head the other way, and pretended to be asleep. Again and again, almost involuntarily, she half rose, remembering the last of the whiskey, but as often lay down again, loathing the cause of her headache.

Stronger and stronger grew her unwillingness to face her son. She had so thoroughly proved herself unfit to be trusted! She began to feel toward him as she had sometimes felt toward her mother when she had been naughty. She began to see that she could make her peace, with him or with herself, only by acknowledging her weakness. Aided by her misery, she had begun to perceive that she could not trust herself, and ought to submit to be treated as the poor creature she was. She had resented the idea that she could not keep herself from drink if she pleased, for she knew she could; but she had not pleased! How could she ever ask him to trust her again!

It is an unfailing surprise when anyone, especially anyone who has always seemed without strength of character, turns round and changes. The only thing Mrs. Gordon then knew as helping her was the strong hand of her son upon her, and the consciousness that had her husband lived, she could never have given way as she had. But there was another help which is never wanting where it can find an entrance; and now first she began to pray, "Lead me not into temptation."

There was one excuse which David alone knew to make for her—that her father was a hard drinker, and his father before him.

Doubtless, during all the period of her excesses, the soul of the woman in her better moments had been ashamed to know her as the thing she was. To drink whiskey, till she did not know what she did next, could not subscribe to her idea of a lady, poor as that idea was. And when the sleeping woman God made wakes up to see in what a house she lives, she will soon grasp at besom and bucket, nor cease her cleansing while spot is left on wall or ceiling or floor. How the waking comes, who can tell! God knows what He wants us to do, and what we can do, and how to help us.

The next morning, Mrs. Gordon came down to breakfast, and finding her son already seated at the table, came up behind him, without a word set the bottle with the last glass of whiskey in it before him, went to her place at the table, gave him one sorrowful look, and sat down.

His heart understood, and answered with a throb of joy so great that he knew it first as pain.

Neither spoke until breakfast was almost over. Then Francis said, "You've grown so much younger, mother, it is quite time you took to riding again! I've been buying a horse for you. Remembering the sort of pony you bought for me, I thought I should like to try whether I could not please you with a horse of my buying."

"Silly boy!" she returned, with a rather pitiful laugh. "Do you suppose at my age I'm going to make a fool of myself on horseback? You forget I'm an old woman!"

"Not a bit of it, mother! If ever you rode as David Barclay says you did, I don't see why you shouldn't ride still. He's a splendid creature! David told me you liked a big fellow. Just put on your habit, mammy, and we'll take a gallop across, and astonish the old man a bit."

"My dear boy, I have no nerve! I'm not the woman I was! It's my own fault, I know, and I'm both sorry and ashamed."

"We are both going to try to be good, mother dear!" faltered Francis.

The poor woman pressed her handkerchief with both hands to her face, and wept for a few moments in silence, then rose and left the room. In an hour she was ready, and out looking for Francis. Her habit was a little too tight for her, but wearable enough. The horses were sent for, and they mounted.

CHAPTER THIRTY-NINE

Two Horsewomen

At Corbyknowe there was a young, well-bred horse which David had himself reared, and Kirsty had been teaching him to carry a lady. Her hostess in Edinburgh, discovering that she was fond of riding and that she had no saddle, had made her a present of her own. She had not used it for many years, but it was in very good condition, and none the worse for being a little old-fashioned. That same morning Kirsty had put on a blue riding habit which Lady Macintosh had given her, and was out on the highest slope of the farm, hoping to catch a sight of the two on horseback together, and so learn that her scheme was a success. She had been on the outlook for about an hour, when she saw them coming along between the castle and Corbyknowe, and went straight for a certain point in the road so as to reach it simultaneously with them. For she had just spied a chance of giving Gordon the opportunity which her father had told her he was longing for, of saying something about her to his mother.

"Who can that be?" said Mrs. Gordon as they trotted gently along, when she spied the lady on horseback. "She rides well! But she seems to be alone! Is there really nobody with her?"

As she spoke, the young horse came over a dry stane dyke in fine style.

"Why, she's an accomplished horsewoman!" exclaimed Mrs.

Gordon. "She must be a stranger! There's not a lady within thirty miles of Weelset can ride like that!"

"Not such a stranger as you think, mother!" rejoined Francis. "That's Kirsty Barclay of Corbyknowe."

"Never, Francis! The girl rides like a lady!"

Francis smiled, perhaps a little triumphantly. Something like what lay in his smile the mother read in it, for it roused at once both her jealousy and her pride. *Her* son to fall in love with a girl that was not even a lady! A Gordon of Weelset to marry a tenant's daughter! Impossible!

Kirsty was now in the road before them, riding slowly in the same direction. It was the progress, however, not the horse that was slow. His frolics, especially when the other horses drew near, kept his rider sufficiently occupied.

Mrs. Gordon quickened her pace, and passed without turning her head or looking at her, but so close, and with so sudden a rush that Kirsty's horse half wheeled and bounded over the dyke by the roadside. Her rudeness annoyed her son, and he jumped his horse into the field and joined Kirsty, letting his mother ride on, and contenting himself with keeping her in sight. After a few moments' talk, however, he proposed that they should overtake her, and cutting off a great loop of the road, they passed her at speed, and turned and met her. She had by this time got a little over her temper, and was prepared to behave with propriety, which meant the dignity becoming her.

"What a lovely horse you have, Miss Barclay!" she said, without other greeting. "How much do you want for him?"

"He is but half-broken," answered Kirsty, "or I would offer to change with you. I almost wonder you look at him—from the back of your own!"

"He is a beauty—is he not? This is my first trial of him. The laird gave me him only this morning. He is as quiet as a lamb."

"There, Donal," said Kirsty to her horse, "take example by yer betters! Jist look hoo he stands! The laird has a true eye for a horse, ma'am," she went on, "but he always says you gave it him."

"Always! Hm!" said Mrs. Gordon to herself, but she looked

kindly at her son.

"How did you learn to ride so well, Kirsty?" she asked.

"I suppose I got it from my father, ma'am! I began with the cows."

"Ah, how is old David?" returned Mrs. Gordon. "I have seen him once or twice about the castle of late but have not spoken to him."

"He is very well, thank you. Will you not come up to the Knowe and rest a moment? My mother will be very glad to see you."

"Not today, Kirsty. I haven't been on horseback for years, and am already tired. We shall turn here. Good morning!"

"Good morning, ma'am! Good-bye, Mr. Gordon!" said Kirsty cheerfully, as she wheeled her horse to set him straight at a steep grassy brae.

CHAPTER FORTY

The Laird and His Mother

The laird and his mother sat and watched Kirsty as her horse tore up the brae.

"She can ride, can't she, mother?" said Francis.

"Well enough for a commoner," answered Mrs. Gordon.

"She rides to please her horse now, but she'll have him as quiet as yours before long," rejoined her son, both a little angry and a little amused at her being called a commoner who was to him like an angel grown young with aeonian life.

"Yes," resumed his mother, as if she *would* be fair, "she does ride well! If only she were a lady, that I might ask her to ride with me! After all it's none of my business what she is—so long as *you* don't want to marry her!" she concluded, with an attempt at laugh.

"But I do want to marry her, mother!" rejoined Francis.

A short year before, his mother would have said what was in her heart, and it would not have been pleasant to hear. But now she was afraid of her son, and was silent; but it only added to her torture that she must be silent. To be dethroned in Castle Weelset by the daughter of one of her own tenants, for as such she thought of them, was indeed galling. "The impudent queen!" she said to herself. "She's ridden on her horse into the heart of the laird!" But for the wholesome consciousness of her own shame, which she felt that her son was always sparing, she would have raged like a fury.

"You that might have had any lady in the land!" she said at length.

"If I might, mother, it would be just as vain to look for her equal."

"You might at least have shown your mother the respect of choosing a lady to sit in her place! You drive me from the house!"

"Mother," said Francis, "I have twice asked Kirsty Barclay to be my wife, and she has twice refused me."

"You may try her again. She had her reasons! She never meant to let you slip! If you got disgusted with her afterward, she would always have her refusal of you to throw in your teeth."

Francis laid his hand on his mother's, and stopped her horse.

"Mother, you compel me!" he said. "When I came home ill and, as I thought, dying, you called me bad names, and drove me from the house. Kirsty found me in a hole in the earth, actually dying then, and saved my life."

"Good heavens, Francis! Are you mad still? How dare you tell such horrible falsehoods of your own mother? You went straight to Corbyknowe!"

"Ask Mrs. Bremner if I speak the truth. She ran out after me, but could not catch me. You drove me out, and if you do not know it now, you do not need to be told how it is that you have forgotten it."

She knew what he meant, and was silent.

"Then Kirsty went to Edinburgh, to Sir Haco Macintosh, and with his assistance brought me to my right mind. If it were not for Kirsty, I should be in my grave, or wandering the earth a maniac. Even alive and well as I am, I should not be with you now had she not shown me my duty."

"I thought as much! All this tyranny of yours, all your late insolence to your mother, comes from the power of that lowborn woman over you! I declare to you, Francis Gordon, if you marry her, I will leave the house."

He made her no answer, and they rode the rest of the way in silence. But in that silence things grew clearer to him. Why should he take pains to persuade his mother to a consent which she had no right to withhold? His desire was altogether reasonable. Why should its fulfillment depend on the unreason of one who had not strength to order her own behavior?

When he had helped her from the saddle, he would have remounted and ridden at once to Corbyknowe, but feared leaving her. She shut herself in her room till she could bear her own company no longer, and then went to the drawing room, where Francis read to her, and played several games of backgammon with her.

Soon after dinner she retired, saying her ride had wearied her, and the moment Francis knew she was in bed, he got his horse, and galloped to the Knowe.

CHAPTER FORTY-ONE

The Coronation

When he arrived, there was no light in the house—all had gone to rest. Unwilling to disturb the father and mother, he rode quietly to the back of the house, where Kirsty's room looked upon the garden. He called her softly. In a moment she peeped out, then opened her window.

"Could ye come doon a minute, Kirsty?" said Francis.

"I'll be wi' ye in less time," she replied, and he had hardly more than dismounted, when she was by his side.

He told her what had passed between him and his mother since she left them.

"It's a real bonny night!" said Kirsty. "And we'll jist take oor time to turn the thing over—that is, if ye be no tired, Francie. Come, we'll put the beastie up first."

She led the horse into the dark stable, took his bridle off, put a halter on him, slackened his girths, and gave him a feed of corn—all in the dark. Then she and Francis set out for the Horn.

The whole night seemed thinking of the day that was gone. All doing seemed at an end, even God Himself to be resting and thinking. The peace of it sank into their hearts and filled them so that they walked a long way without speaking. There was no wind, and no light but the starlight. The air was like the clear dark inside some diamonds. The only sound that broke the stillness as they went was the voice of Kirsty, sweet and low, and it was as if the dim starry vault thought, rather than uttered, the words she quoted:

> "Summer Night, come from God,
>   On your beauty, I see
> A still wave has flowed
>   Of Eternity!"

At a certain spot on the ridge of the Horn, Francis stopped.

"This is where ye left me this time last year, Kirsty," he said, "wi' my Maker to make a man o' me. It was almost makin me over again!"

There was a low stone just visible among the heather, and Kirsty seated herself upon it. Francis threw himself among the heather, and lay looking up in her face.

"That mither o' yours is almost over muckle for ye, Francie!" said Kirsty.

"It's no often, Kirsty, ye tell me what I ken as weel's yersell!" returned Francis.

"Weel, Francie, ye must tell me somethin the night! If it wouldna mismove ye, I would fain ken hoo ye went through that day we parted here."

Without a moment's hesitation, Francis began the tale—giving her to know, however, that in what took place there was much he did not understand so as to tell it again.

When he had made an end, Kirsty rose and said, "Would ye please sit upo' that stane, Francie!"

In pure obedience he rose from the heather, and sat upon the stone. She went behind him, and clasped his head, round the temples, with her shapely, strong, faithful hands.

"I ken ye noo for a man, Francis. Ye have set yerself to do *His* will, and no yer own. Ye're a king, and for want o' a better crown, I crown ye wi' my twa hands."

Then she came round in front of him, he sitting bewildered and taking no part in the solemn ceremony save that of submission, and knelt slowly down before him, laying her head on his knees, and saying, "And here's yer kingdom, Francie—my head and my heart! Do wi' me what ye will."

"Come hame wi' me, and help save my mither," he answered, in a voice choked with emotion.

"I will," she said, and would have risen, but he laid his hands on her head, and thus they remained for a time in silence. Then they rose, and went.

They had gone about halfway to the farm before either spoke. Then Kirsty said, "Francie, there's one thing I must beg o' ye and but one, that ye willna desire me to take the head o' yer table. I canna but think it an ungracious thing that a yoong woman like me, the son's wife, should put the man's own mither, his father's wife, oot o' the place where his father set her. I'm laying doon no principle; I'm sayin only hoo I feel. I want to come hame as her doctor, no as mistress o' the hoose in her stead. And ye see, Francie, that'll give ye anither hold o' her, against disgracin o' herself! Promise me, Francie, and I'll soon take most o' the trouble o' her off o' yer hands."

"Ye're aye right, Kirsty!" answered Francis, "As ye will."

The next morning, Kirsty told her parents that she was going to marry Francis.

"Ye do right, my bairn," said her father. "He's come in sight o' 'is high callin, and it's no possible for ye longer to refuse him."

"But, eh! What am I to do wantin ye, Kirsty?" moaned her mother.

"Ye mind, mither," answered Kirsty, "hoo I would be oot the day wi' Steenie, and ye never thought ye hadna me!"

"Na, never. I aye kenned I had the twa o' ye."

"Weel, it's no a God's-innocent but a deevil's-gowk I'll have to look after noo, and I must come hame every possible chance to get heartenin frae you and my father, or I willna be able to bide it. Eh, mither, after Steenie, it'll be awful to spend the day wi' *her!* It's no that ever she'll be tipsy. I shall see to that! It's that she'll aye be empty!"

Here Kirsty turned to her father, and said, "Will ye give me a tocher, father?"

"Ay will I, lassie. What ye like, so far as I have it t' give."

"I want Donal—that's all. Ye see, I must ride a heap wi' the puir thing, and I would fain have somethin aneath me that ye gave me! I would have liked things to bide as they are, but she would have worn puir Francie to the verra death!"

EPILOGUE

Mrs. Gordon managed the house and her reward was to sit at the head of the table. But she paid Kirsty infinitely more for the privilege than any but Kirsty could know, in the form of leisure for things she liked far better than housekeeping.

Among the rest, she discovered such songs as this in her heart.

Love Is Home

Love is the part, and love is the whole;
Love is the robe, and love is the pall;
Ruler of heart and brain and soul,
Love is the lord and the slave of all!
I thank Thee, love, that thou lov'st me;
I thank Thee more that I love thee.

Love is the rain, and love is the air;
Love is the earth that holdeth fast;
Love is the root that is buried there,
Love is the open flower at last!
I thank thee, love all round about,
That the eyes of my love are looking out.

218 Heather and Snow

Love is the sun, and love is the sea;
Love is the tide that comes and goes;
Flowing and flowing it comes to me;
Ebbing and ebbing to thee it flows!
Oh my sun, and my wind, and tide!
My sea, and my shore, and all beside!

Light, oh light that art by showing;
Wind, oh wind that liv'st by motion;
Thought, oh thought that art by knowing;'
Will, that art born in self-devotion!
Love is you, though not all of you know it;
Ye are not love, yet ye always show it!

Faithful Creator, heart-longed-for Father,
Home of our heart-infolded brother,
Home to Thee all Thy glories gather—
All are Thy love, and there is no other!
O Love-at-rest; we loves that roam—
Home unto Thee, we are coming home!

The End

WORD LIST

aeonian	lasting for a long time
aye	always
bete noir	bugbear, source of irritation
brae	bank
byre	cow barn
catastroff	catastophe
deal	a wooden board
drappy	drop
drystane dyke	drystone wall
factor	broker
fain	eager
fell (adj.)	sharp
fleg	a fright
fleyt	afraid
frae	from
gangrel	vagrant
gerse	grass
gowk	fool
guid	good
kelpie	water spirit
ken	know
kirk	church
langsyne	long ago
losh	oh my!
midge	small insect
muckle	much
nor	than

sic	such
siller	cellar
stane	stone
sward	turf
theroot	thereout, out there
til	to
tocher	dowry
wale	whip wound
whiles	sometimes
winsey	woven linen and wool
won	crept
worset	closely twisted yarn
yowie	baby ewe, term of endearment

Fiction From Victor Books

George MacDonald

A Quiet Neighborhood
The Seaboard Parish
The Vicar's Daughter
The Shopkeeper's Daughter
The Last Castle
The Prodigal Apprentice
On Tangled Paths
Heather and Snow

Cliff Schimmels

Winter Hunger
Rivals of Spring
Summer Winds
Rites of Autumn

Donna Fletcher Crow

Brandley's Search
To Be Worthy
A Gentle Calling
Something of Value

Robert Wise

The Pastors' Barracks
The Scrolls of Edessa